Season of Secrets

Esoteric Equinox
~ Book 1 ~

Kerry E. B. Black

Season
of Secrets

Esoteric Equinox - Book I

Kerry E. B. Black

RhetAskew  Publishing

United States of America

COVER ILLUSTRATION
& INTERIOR DESIGN

© 2018 – FLITTERBOW PRODUCTIONS
AND RHETASKEW PUBLISHING

ISBN-13: 978-1-949398-17-5
ISBN-10: 1-949398-17-X

Dedication

Dedicated to my Angel of a mother, Beverly Virginia, who is nothing like Casey's mother, and with special thanks to my sister Heather and my nieces Megan and Grace who encouraged, read, and made suggestions.

This book would not be possible without the watchful editing and careful guidance of Emma Gitani, and the amazing staff at RhetAskew Publishing. Thank you for your faith in this humble work.

I would be remiss if I didn't thank the many in my writing circles who've helped me along my path, especially C.C. Aune, Elaina Portugal, A.M. Justice, Brightest Nightstar, Angela L. Lindseth, Terry M. West, the Birches of the Circle, and Randall Andrews and his Writers World. And of course, my family.

And a special thanks to all of you who take the time to adventure with Casey and her friends. I do hope you enjoy the discoveries!

Chapter One

First Class of Freshman Year

Casey Adams scrutinized the map sent in the freshman welcome package and gulped. She closed her eyes and calmed her heart beat. *I'm an interloper in the hallowed halls of academia.*

Her heart pounded, and she concentrated to steady her breath. In and out. *You can do this.* She opened her eyes and allowed the rush of people to ruffle her hair. People with purpose. *Why did I think this was a good idea?*

She took another deep breath and controlled its release. *It's so overwhelming.*

The campus bustled with activity and energy. Friends embraced. Book bags hung from students' backs like bright-colored turtle shells. Earbuds leaked an eclectic mix of music. On every cobble-stoned pathway, kids walked toward classrooms and lecture halls. They greeted one another. Some patted the backs of obviously misdirected under-classmen. Even Casey's fellow freshmen, apparent by the nervous twitching of their widened eyes, moved toward something. Casey trembled. *I don't know where to go.*

Casey swallowed a huge lump in her throat. *I can do this.* She smoothed her map, resolved.

The names on the map sounded foreign. Leighster Studies Chamber. Heinsman Hall. Fritzwicky Planetarium. *I could ask directions, I suppose*. Her stomach clenched. *Who do I ask though*? The passing faces seemed focused on individual pursuits. Excited steps, chewed lips, nervous laughter, but no one spared more than a glance at timid nineteen-year-old Casey.

She gulped around another imagined lump, and a glistening glaze of sweat coated her forehead. *Of course, asking directions means I have to actually talk to a person*. A giggle bubbled, but Casey squelched it.

Don't want to be the weirdo insane girl. At least not the first day. Casey balled her hands into fists clenched at her side and nodded. *I worked too hard to get here. Suck it up and figure this out*.

Casey spotted Carlisle Hall and needed the squat building behind. *Should be along this pathway*. She entered the Quad and paused to consult the map. *At least, I think so*. She forced muscles trembling with apprehension into motion.

Along the steps of Old Main, booths of sorority girls speckled the limestone. The girls vied for new pledges. A bubbly girl sing-songed, "Take a flyer. You'll love us!" She thrust the pastel page through the map, tearing it along the fold line. Casey's mouth dropped as the oblivious sorority sister bounced back to her friends.

"See, I gave away the last one!"

Casey gaped with disbelief. Her hands shook as she pieced the map back together, ignoring the pledge party invitation. It fluttered to the ground like a harbinger of autumn leaves. She climbed stairs and studied lecture hall numbers, pleased to make progress.

Right building and—she squinted at the numbers—*right room.*

Proud of her accomplishment, she claimed a middle seat, unloaded her books, and prepared for her first class of freshman year. "Introduction to World Religions" with Dr. Krochalis.

Her classmates entered the room. Some knew one another. Others offered wavering smiles, handshakes, and hopeful expressions.

A fair-haired young man strode to a seat in the anterior, stretched out his long legs and threw his head back in a caricature of repose. He tipped his chair onto its back legs and laced his fingers behind his head. "This will be a snooze-fest," he said with a dramatic sigh.

A slim girl whose overpowering perfume rivaled spring honeysuckle squealed when she saw him. "Devon? Oh, my goodness! I can't believe it! We knew each other in high school. I'm Annemarie. Do you remember me? I tutored you in Spanish."

Devon squinted through overgrown bangs. A half-smile crossed his face. "Sure, I remember. How you doing?"

A smile brightened Annamarie's pretty face.

"Great. I didn't know you were going here. That's so cool." Annemarie flounced into the seat next to him and unzipped her designer book bag. Her pink pen sprouted feathers from the cap, resembling a tiny, deranged flamingo. She twiddled it through her fingers, a fairy wand shedding glitter. She spread out matching folders and a copy of "Interacting with the World Through Religion." With her desktop arranged, she sat with the impeccable posture of a model student.

Casey smiled. A sorority pledge invitation peeked from the bag. *Annemarie would make flawless pledge material. Bubbly. Adorable. Perky perfection.*

Annemarie tapped her pen. "Where are your books, Devon? Am I going to need to tutor you here, too?" She twirled her dark hair around her index finger and blinked through curled lashes.

Devon shrugged. "Didn't buy the book. You know how much it cost?" He laced his fingers behind his head. "Figure I'll borrow yours. You know, we could have study sessions. Late night. Just the two of us."

He leveled a smoldering stare.

Annamarie blushed and giggled. "Sure, that would be fun!"

Oh Lord. Casey looked away, lips pressed into a prim line. *I hate when people act stupid.*

Students took seats, some whispering, some silent, and others were boisterous in their approach to communication. None noticed Casey.

A hush fell when the professor entered the room and took a position behind the lectern. Her voice carried with ease. "I've taught for the past twenty-five years. My approach is simple. I am a conduit. I share my vast understanding of the subject matter. You learn. Or not. The choice is yours." She fixed them with a pointed stare. "The syllabus is online, and you can buy used hard copies of the text in the student bookstore on campus.

"I checked, so none of this nonsense of not being able to afford the curriculum material. College is expensive, my friends. So is life. Get used to it." She tapped a finger against the lectern.

Looks like she's pointing at Devon.

Dr. Krochalis turned a page and cleared her throat. "Assignments are for your benefit. They will help you achieve an understanding of the material presented. They will not be graded, so do them or don't."

Devon was not the only student who whistled at this pronouncement.

Dr. Krochalis removed her spectacles and set them with a tinny click on the podium.

"I'm not your mother. I'm not paying for your classes. Therefore, I don't care if you pass or fail."

The class fell silent, and she shrugged.

"I can tell you from my extensive experience as a professor, student, and teacher, though, that if you do not put in the effort required, your grade will suffer. So, you choose."

She replaced her glasses and continued. "There will be a midterm and final grade. Follow the syllabus, and you will do well. Office hours are posted. Read the assignments. The material we'll cover is deep and interesting. You'll learn about what is universal within us and what defines our differences. You may even come to know yourself better if you apply yourself."

She scanned her students and paused when she came to Casey. *Is she looking at me?* Casey shrunk into her seat.

"In fact, there are opportunities to participate in various religious ceremonies in these parts. A lucky few of you will find yourselves invited. Avail yourself of opportunities such as the Equinox ceremony, and you very well may find yourself on the path of real discovery and self-actualization."

She slapped a hand atop her papers and waved. "That's all for this session. Refer to your syllabus and read the introduction and chapter one. There are discussion points highlighted on the syllabus. Be prepared to explore your understanding of the material you've read. Until then, adieu. We'll meet again Wednesday."

Nobody moved.

Dr. Krochalis flapped her hands and shooed them. "Go on. Enjoy the rest of the morning. Work begins in earnest when next we meet. Until then, class dismissed."

Casey remained still as fellow students stowed away their books and writing implements. *Short class.* She glanced at the syllabus. Introduction and chapter one of the tome due Wednesday. *Wonder how long the chapters are?* She opened the book. Fresh ink, and the binding creaked like arthritic joints. About fifty pages. She sighed. *Joy.*

A controlled roar echoed through the lecture hall as students exited. Devon typed his number into Annemarie's cell phone.

Dr. Krochalis ran a hand through her short-cropped hair. Sprays of silver and steel fell into place with its passage. She nodded as students passed.

Reminds me of Aunt Hettie. Don't know why. She looks nothing like Aunt Hettie.

Among her family members, only Aunt Hettie had encouraged Casey to attend school. "You should go to college. You're smart. Don't waste your life." She slipped money from her waitressing apron into Casey's reluctant grip.

Casey leapt from her seat as the lectern fell with a resounding crash. She rushed down the stairway to help.

When she lifted the heavy oaken piece, her fingers sunk into its intricate carvings. Stars encircled moons wrapped with vines and hearts. She gathered the professor's scattered papers. Mythical monsters stared, baleful from ivory parchment. Restless spirits whirled over the pages with fascinating grace.

"Thank you," Dr. Krochalis said with a sheepish smile. "Bumped the darned thing over. Happens all the time." She patted her copious hips and laughed. "Jean Krochalis." She extended her hand.

Casey pushed the pile of papers into the outstretched hand. She studied her scuffed sneakers muddied from chasing her little sister and brother around the back yard.

The professor asked, "And you are?"

Casey's mouth dropped but produced no sound. *I'm not used to attention, especially from an authority figure.* She cleared her throat. *Spent most of my life invisible.*

She glanced through her disheveled hair. *Still, this is a chance to start anew, right?* "Casey Adams, ma'am," she whispered to Dr. Krochalis' black ballet-influenced flats. Little silver ribbons adorned their tops. *Cute.*

"Very nice to meet you, Ms. Adams. I look forward to getting to know you better."

Casey did not detect sarcasm. *Wish she'd stop looking at me, though.*

She nodded before the rising blush engulfed her face. She gathered her backpack, hunched to support its weight, and rushed to find the next class.

Casey shielded her eyes from the dazzling afternoon sun. People rushed to their classes. Some bounced like Tigger. Others slumped over their books, engulfed with their private concerns.

Once in the stream of activity, Casey found comfort on a bench beneath a maple tree. She pulled her knees to her chest and willed their boney presence to compose her erratic heartbeat. *Why can't I be normal?*

She closed her eyes to the bustle around her and focused on the buzz of a nearby bee. Its hum calmed her, nature's metronome. Her heartbeat matched the relaxing rhythm. The bee concerned itself with its tasks and ignored distractions.

Casey, be like a bee. She imagined musical notes dancing in golden sprays, glittering in the darkness behind her eyelids. Her breathing slowed until her chest rose and fell with a steady rhythm.

I can do this. I can be a college student. Can't I?

Chapter Two

A New Acquaintance

A girl sat beside Casey. Her eyes conjured images of lazy afternoons picnicking lakeside, breezes dancing over the waters. An open, easy smile stretched across her freckled face. "Sure, is crazy here, isn't it?" The girl extended her hand. "Hi. I'm Jaimie. I saw you in Dr. K's class. The syllabus looks intense, doesn't it?"

Casey blinked. *She saw me*? *Nobody ever sees me.* "Uh, I guess. I don't really know what to expect."

"Freshman, huh?"

Casey nodded.

"It gets easier." Jaimie fiddled with the zipper on her backpack and pulled out her schedule.

"Hope so."

"So, what did you think of Dr. Krochalis?"

Casey creased her brow. "Pardon?"

"You talked with her, right? Helped her pick up papers?"

Those papers were a bit disturbing. Casey gasped. *This girl was watching me.*

"I heard she's a hoot. Has students to her house and stuff. Literary luncheons and that sort of thing."

Casey shrugged. "I just picked up some papers."

Jaimie smoothed her schedule against her knee. "I've got Intro to Psych with Bridges next. You?"

"Um," Casey consulted her memory of the schedule she'd studied for the past week. Psychology 101 followed Comparative Religion. "Yeah. Me, too."

Jaimie stuffed her schedule into her laden backpack.

"Cool. We can walk together."

Walk together? Casey's head buzzed, overwhelmed. *Who's this girl, and why is she so friendly?*

Jaimie stood with a smile. "What's your name, by the way?"

She saw me, she's talking to me, and she wants to know my name. Unprecedented.

Casey stared at the halo formed by the sun streaming through the girl's hair. *Beautiful. She could model for a Renaissance painting of a saint.*

The girl widened her eyes.

She's waiting for an answer. "Oh, Casey."

"O'Casey? Are you Irish?" Jaimie laughed.

Casey stiffened when Jamie threw a conspiratorial arm around her shoulder. "Just teasing. Let's set off, huh? Don't want to be late for our class."

Jaimie pointed at a modern building. It contrasted with the gray stone and classic architecture of the majority of the buildings. "That's where they host comedy acts and bands on weekends. We'll have to go together, okay? During the summer, we ate picnics by the lake. Pretty, but lots of mosquitos. Do you mind bugs? If you don't mind them, we can eat there sometime." She took a deep breath and launched into another diatribe. "Do you know that's a man-made lake? One of the previous Deans installed it for his wife. She was sad about leaving her home, so he had the lake dug in the shape of her home state. You can see it from above. The view up on the bluff over there is great, or from the Dean's office." She pointed to a window in the administration building. "Kind of romantic, don't you think?"

"Guess so," Casey said. *She seems to know the history of the entire campus.*

"Say, what dorm are you in?" She didn't wait for the answer. "I'm in Bly Women's. Isn't it weird that there are no co-ed dorms here? Something about the Amish giving the land and insisting on the separation between men and women. That's why the boys' dorms are across the campus."

She spun and pointed. "They have further to walk. I bet it will suck in the winter. The RA's are strict about visitors, too. So what dorm are you in?"

Casey cleared her throat. *Not used to so much attention, so much talking. I've always been the invisible girl at school.* She swallowed and licked her lips. Her eyes jumped from a tree limb to an airplane high in the clouds, to a splinter in a wooden bench, but her vision refused to alight on any one thing. She shrugged. "I commute."

"Seriously? I don't live far from here, but I wanted to get away from home for a bit. Enjoy campus life." She wrinkled her nose and grimaced. "Not quite what I expected, though. So, where do you live?"

Casey adjusted her backpack as unaccustomed to its burden as she was to conversation outside her family. "Not far. About a half hour away unless I get stuck behind a hay wagon."

Jaimie laughed. "Yeah, they don't move very fast, do they?"

Before she knew it, Casey traversed the campus and entered Dr. Bridge's classroom. Jamie continued chatting as she chose and took a seat. Casey sat beside her and set up her desk. Note paper to the right, pen atop, book and clinical notebook to the left.

Jaimie asked, "You are a bit OCD, aren't you?"

Casey chewed her lower lip and studied the desktop. *This is all too much.* She hummed. *Does she ever stop talking?*

"Casey?" Jaimie leaned into Casey's field of vision. "Are you okay?"

The incessant chatter filled up her head. *It is nice to have someone to talk to though. This is normal, I think.* "I just need a few minutes. Overwhelmed, you know?"

"I get that." Jaimie reclined in her seat and stretched her legs. "This is my second semester. I started in the summer. Think I said that already though. Not many people here then, but it let me know how to get around. That helps."

Heat rose in Casey's cheeks. She rubbed her temples with her thumbs. *Breathe in and out, slow and measured.*

"Yeah, you know, I have a theory," Jaimie said. "I think we meet people for a reason."

"A reason?"

"Yeah. Like you don't know anyone yet, so you met me. Good luck, huh?" Jaimie chuckled. "Don't look so worried. I don't bite." She tapped her desktop with the palms of her hands. "Hey, do you have a big family?"

Casey thought of her little sister, Rachel, and baby brother, Malcolm. *Baby. Not anymore. He's six this month. Then there's the pillar of the family, Rob, who left when he graduated. We almost never hear from him. Thanks for the help, big brother. Mom's sick and Dad works all the time. What a life.*

Jaimie studied Casey's face. *Wish she would stop staring at me.*

Jaimie did not wait for an answer. "I have a brother. His name is James. He's my twin, but we don't look at all the same. Fraternals, you know? Same womb, different eggs. James has autism." Jaimie's eyes danced with friendship.

Casey chewed a strand of her hair. The crunch between her teeth soothed.

Jaimie remained silent until classmates filed in with the reckless abandon of threshold youth. She leaned close and whispered, "I think we're going to be great friends. What do you think?"

Sure, we'll be great friends until you meet my crazy family and realize how wacky I am, too.

Casey stretched a strained smile and cleared her throat, but Dr. Bridges' arrival prevented her from voicing an answer.

Chapter Three

Lunch in the Willows

Dr. Bridges scrawled his name across the bottom of a white board and faced the class. "How many of you plan to enter psychology?"

A few students, including Jaimie, raised their hands. "The rest of you are here because this fills a humanities elective. The course is a good overview of complex material. For those of you interested in the complicated workings of the human mind, this is an excellent place for you. For any unfortunates who enrolled in this class with the erroneous belief this would be a simple course, you are sadly mistaken. Ours is a noble lineage." He wrote **Sigmund Freud** on the top of the board. "Even the thickest of you has undoubtedly heard this name. The father of modern psychological study had a famous student."

He drew a line from Freud and wrote **Carl Jung**. "Jung explored the collective unconscious and interpreted dreams as a way of understanding a person's psychological state."

Beneath Jung, he wrote another name. "This was one of Jung's prized students. He taught me. I'm teaching you. Thus, you can say with authority that your psychological studies are direct descendants of Sigmund Freud himself."

Jaimie whistled through her teeth. She whispered, "That's fabulous."

He smiled up at Jaimie. "Indeed. However, that leaves a lot for you to live up to."

Great acoustics here, I guess. He's looking right at us. Casey gulped. Dr. Bridges embodied everything she imagined in a young academician: a full, wavy head of hair, perfect teeth, a well-trimmed mustache, and a physique that filled out his tweed suit.

When he returned to his lecture, Jaimie leaned close to whisper, "Well, I'll be looking forward to this class."

Casey blushed. "That's what I was thinking, too."

The girls giggled until Dr. Bridges threw them a glare. Casey composed herself with upright posture and steady, attentive gaze, but laughter bubbled under the facade.

Even upset, Dr. Bridges is really cute. Her lips quivered.

Dr. Bridges said, "Locked within the mind are secrets few are brave enough to explore. If you plumb the depths, you may discover your own potential and better comprehend the world."

Sounds like the aim of Dr. Krochalis' class, too. Funny how so many things are related.

As she jotted notes and listened to the lecture, all thoughts of humor abated.

Dr. Bridges straightened his notecards with a hasty thump against the lectern. "In conclusion, in this class, if you apply yourself, you'll learn surprising things about yourselves and your habits. Why you do what you do. We'll discuss nature versus nurture and freedom of choice as opposed to the dictates of genetic predisposition. Can we escape the coding of our very existence? Can we master monsters hidden within?" He swept the room with a serious expression. "Refer to the syllabus. Do the readings so that you'll be prepared. During our next class we'll plunge into the primordial pool to seek the ultimate satisfaction."

Casey waited until classmates filed out then gathered her things. *Face monsters within? Does he mean madness?*

When she'd stowed the last of her pencils, Jaimie grabbed her hand. "Oh, that was fun! I am so glad we have Dr. Bridges' class together. What's next?"

"I have an hour before Physics 101."

"I have two before my next course. Let's get some lunch at the Willows."

Casey considered the five-dollar bill in her wallet. "Is it expensive?"

"Nah, it's for college kids. Everyone knows we're poor and hungry." Jaimie threw back her head and laughed as she guided Casey along a white-stone path to the basement of Andrews Hall.

Dark and cramped described the Willows. Medieval tapestries hung from stone walls, like a tavern from a fantasy novel. The waitresses wore low-cut white blouses cinched at the waist by wide black belts in pirate wench fashion.

Jaimie watched Casey's reaction. "It's as fun as a Renaissance Faire in here, isn't it?"

Casey stammered, "Sort of." *Never been to a Renaissance Faire.* She hunched from the low ceiling. *This place kind of reminds me of a cave, actually.* Despite her diminutive stature, the walls curved toward Casey.

"This is the kind of place I could see Aragorn drinking a tankard. Oh, wait, have you read Tolkien?"

Casey said, "Sure." *Lord of the Rings, The Hobbit, and The Silmarillion.*

Jaimie's broad smile lit her face. "Oh, I knew we had tons in common! There's a course called 'Unlocking Tolkien,' offered by one of the monk professors. He's really old and technically retired, but he allows only two dozen students in his classes once a year. I'm on the waiting list. Maybe you can ask your advisor, and we can take it together."

"Maybe."

A waitress delivered a sizzling plate of fajitas to a nearby table, and Casey's stomach grumbled.

Jaimie giggled. "Wait 'til you taste the food. It's good."

They slid into a corner booth. Casey tipped the menu toward a candle in the center of the table to read and make a selection. She pointed to the menu picture when the waitress collected the order.

"I'll have a Willow burger platter, please. Medium well. Water to drink."

Jaimie ordered the wurst platter and a soda and then resumed prattling about college life. "Are you going to pledge a sorority?"

Casey blanched and shook her head.

"Me either. Not my scene, you know? I want something more profound from life, something deeper than discussing nail polish shades and makeup trends."

Casey furrowed her brow. "I thought sororities raise money for charities and stuff."

Jaimie shrugged. "Some do, I guess, and that's nice. I'm just not into the whole stereotype, though. Pretty in pink conformity. That's what bothers me most."

The door opened, and a group of leather-clad men walked in.

Jaimie leapt and rushed toward a tall, dark-haired man. "Oh my gosh! Ryan. I'm so glad to see you. You have to meet my new friend."

She hugged his arm and pulled him to their booth.

Ryan's half smile spoke of amusement. He nodded to his friends. One of the men smiled, and Casey looked away. The friends took seats around a long, wooden table.

"Ryan, this is Casey. Casey, this is Ryan. I met Ryan in experimental arts over the summer. He's crazy talented. Today is Casey's first day. She's cool. You'll like her." She slid into the booth and pulled him with her.

"Nice to meet you, Casey. How do you enjoy it so far here at Old NorEast U?"

Casey sunk into the bench and willed the shadows to engulf her. She whispered, "It's fine."

Jaimie threw an arm about Casey's shoulders and crushed against her. "Casey's a bit shy. She'll warm up, though, if you're nice."

Ryan's grin made a crooked ascent. "Well, love, I'm very nice." He wiggled his eyebrows and laughed.

His friends called, "Ryan, what do you want to eat?"

"Gotta go, girls. Lunch and all." He slid out, then leaned his elbows on the table. "Say, if you're not busy Wednesday night, why don't you two come to our performance? The band's playing at seven."

Jaimie clapped. "Oh, we'll be there. Thanks."

Jaimie watched his retreating form. She whispered, "Isn't he divine?"

Casey considered his angular features. Tight blue jeans accentuated his thin waist. *Skinnier than me, I think.* His long waves fell between his shoulder blades. He walked with aloof confidence. *Dr. Bridges is much more handsome.* She shrugged. "I guess." She stole a glance at the man who'd smiled and hid a gasp. He tipped his smiling head and winked before he returned his attention to Ryan and his friends. *Now, he's pretty darn cute, though.*

Jaimie grabbed her hands. "You just have to come with me on Wednesday. Promise you won't leave me hanging."

Casey's heart began an irregular pattern, too fast for comfort. "I might have something else to do."

Jaimie squeezed her hands. "Oh, please? I can't go alone. They'd think of me as a desperate groupie or something. Come on, be a pal."

I want a pal. "Let me see what's going on at home." *Something's always going on at home.*

"Okay." Jaimie bounced in her seat. "I'm so excited. We're going to have the best time!" She hugged Casey, who froze in her embrace.

The waitress brought their food and set a pitcher of water and pewter tankards on the table. "Enjoy," she said.

Casey chewed her burger, savoring the flavors, while Jaimie gushed about Ryan and the band.

"They're called Stages of Grief. They do old-time classic metal covers."

Casey relaxed into the rhythm of her speech, finding comfort in its ebbs and flows but not entirely taking in the meaning of the conversation.

Casey smiled and nodded when Jaimie paused.

"Well?" Jaimie asked, eyebrows raised.

Casey replayed the conversation. *Music. What kind did she like?* "You'll laugh. I have a kid sister who loves pop and boy bands, so I hear that a lot. My little brother likes little kids stuff, but he's in elementary school, so..."

Jaimie laughed. "That's all well and good, but do you like?"

Casey shrugged. "Like I said, you'll laugh."

Jaimie's smile disappeared. "I won't."

"I listen to quiet stuff when I'm driving by myself."

Jaimie's lips quivered. "Like easy listening?"

Casey's mouth dropped open, and she pointed at Jaimie. "You promised not to laugh." *Gosh, she reminds me of Rachel.* She bit back a laugh of her own.

"No, I listen to classical, like Bach and Vivaldi."

"Oh." Jaimie lifted her napkin and pantomimed waving to a crowd.

"Well, la ti dah."

Casey swiped the napkin, crumpled it into a ball, and tossed it atop the table. "So much for your promises."

Jaimie surprised Casey with another hug. "Nah, it's cool. Who doesn't like the classics?"

Casey paid her tab, and Jaimie guided her to her next class. "See you tomorrow, and don't forget about Wednesday night, okay?"

Casey nodded, bemused.

Chapter Four

Welcome Home

Casey hummed along with Vivaldi's "Seasons" during her drive home. Trees dotted bright spots of yellow and orange among the green of early autumn.

Casey caressed the steering wheel. *I love driving.* She pressed deeper into her seat. *When I'm driving, I'm in control of something powerful.*

The driveway gravel grumbled as she pulled up to her house. Dark clouds skittered across the steely sky and threatened a thunderstorm. The ozone-heavy air buzzed with cricket song as she climbed her house's worn back steps.

The screen door squealed an announcement of "someone's pushing me again." Two voices sing-songed, "Hi, Casey!" Her little brother and sister giggled under the patio table.

She knelt to see them better. "What are you doing?"

Ten-year-old Rachel climbed out and hugged her sister. "How was your first day at school?"

Casey kissed her head and rested her chin atop Rachel's soft hair. "It was interesting. I have some really cool classes, and I met a nice girl who wants to be my friend."

"That's good. Any cute guys?"

"You're boy crazy, you know?"

Rachel snorted. "Am not."

Malcolm army-crawled from beneath a chair. "Sure, you are." His mischievous smile highlighted his first missing tooth.

Casey lifted his chin. "Did that wiggler finally come out?"

"Yep. Guess the toof fairy's coming tonight."

"Guess so." *Great. And I spent all of my money on lunch.* "Can I see it?"

Rachel wrinkled her nose. "Ewe, it's gross. It has a bloody root attached."

Malcolm rushed from the room with a yell. "Be right back."

Casey smiled. *Six-year-olds don't walk. They don't sit still. They run, hop, and wiggle.*

Rachel slipped an arm around Casey's waist.

Casey looked into her sister's face. "How'd it go today?"

Rachel shrugged and stretched a strained smile. "All right I guess."

"School starts in two weeks." Casey stretched her own smile, her muscles mutinying. *Why's our life so weird?* "Everything should be better then."

"For you and me it will be better," Rachel said.

She blinked as though dust settled in her eyes. "But what about for Malcolm?"

Casey creased her brow. "What do you mean? He starts kindergarten the same day you head to sixth. You'll take the bus together, right?"

Rachel pressed her lips into a tight line. She whispered, "Mom decided Malcolm should stay home to help her. She said he's not ready for school."

Casey lost her breath for a moment. "I don't understand. I already enrolled him." Electricity coursed through her, energy pooling at her joints, leaving her nauseated.

Darn it, what are you playing at, Mom?

Rachel's head hung. "Mom said you didn't have the right to do it. She unenrolled him."

Casey's mouth hung slack. "But Dad asked me to take care of the paperwork. I took Malcolm for his admission interview and placement tests. We met the teacher, Mrs. Hemshaw. She's really nice, and Malcolm liked her."

I'll talk to Dad when he gets home from work tonight.

The screen door slammed as Malcolm rushed, his tooth in the outstretched palm of his hand, a pampered prince presenting an engagement ring.

Casey whistled. "Wow-wee! That came out of your mouth? It looks pretty, like a tiny pearl."

He bounced from foot to foot. "Do you think the toof fairy will like it?"

Casey examined it. "No cavities. It's a beautiful specimen. I think the tooth fairy will be proud to add this to her collection. Let's put it in the tooth fairy pillow so it doesn't get lost, okay?"

The siblings held hands as they walked inside, though Malcolm skipped.

A quivery voice froze their progress. "Why are you so loud? You know I have a headache. I told you I have a headache. Is Casey home?"

"I'm here, Mom." She motioned to the back stairwell. Rachel guided Malcolm up.

"Why are you allowing them to run around, acting noisy as hooligans?" Mom propped on the couch swathed in a satin robe, slippers at the ready close at hand. She resembled a disheveled queen among the cushions. The soft throw blanket slid to puddle on the floor. A pitcher of lemonade and a selection of snacks sat at the ready on a nearby side table.

Casey lingered in the doorway. *Don't want to get too close. She seems a bit off today.* She whispered, "They're kids, Mom."

"I know they're kids. I'm not stupid. They need to know how to mind their mother though."

"They try. We all do. I'll take them upstairs

and play a game. You rest."

Her voice sounded like a growl. "Oh no you don't. Where's dinner? I'm hungry."

Guess it's a bad day. "Okay. What do you want for dinner?"

Casey dodged a tissue box. It bounced off the wall near her head. "Don't get smart with me. Why didn't you bring something? You were out."

Casey gulped. "I'm sorry, Mom. I didn't have any money to buy anything. I'll put something together and tell the kids to stay quiet."

"Where were you, anyway?"

She blinked back tears. *Nothing I do matters, really.* "I was at school. First day."

"Don't lie. You graduated."

"College, Mom. First day of freshman year. Old Nor'East. Don't you remember?"

"How did you get in to college? Who's paying for it?"

The words fell like slaps across her face. "I did, and I am. I'll get dinner together. You rest." She hurried into the kitchen, ahead of threatened tears. She clenched her fists and bit her lip.

I'm not going to cry. Not now.

She took deep breaths to compose her voice and dialed her phone. "Hi, Daddy. How's your day?"

With his voice as comforting as bedtime stories, he said, "Casey girl! My brilliant scholar. How was your first day of college?"

At these words, the sting of her mother's tirade slipped away. She closed her eyes, grateful. "Good. It was good. When will you be home?"

"I don't get off until nine, so nine-thirty, the way I usually do."

"Such long days, Daddy. I don't think they're good for you."

He sighed, his voice tired and wary. "It's how I bring home the bacon. What's going on there?"

"Same stuff. I'm making dinner. I'll put something in the microwave for you."

"Good deal."

"Oh, Malcolm lost his first tooth. Daddy, I don't have any cash. Can you please bring something from the tooth fairy?"

A pause. "Sure."

"Great. By the way, did you know Mom unenrolled him from school?"

Another sigh. "We'll talk about it when I get home."

"Sure. Don't forget the tooth fairy money."

"See you when I get there."

Chapter Five

Tooth Fairy

After a dinner of grilled cheese sandwiches, apple slices, and reheated tomato soup, Casey and the kids cleaned up and retired upstairs for a board game. Malcolm ran in enthusiastic circles when he won.

"Shh." Rachel frowned. "Malcolm, do you want to upset Mom?"

Malcolm glanced around as though a Boogy Man might claim him. He wiggled. "I was happy."

Pity we can't share happy in our house, or we might upset Mom.

She oversaw his bedtime preparations and tucked him in for the night with a kiss.

"I can't wait to see what the toof fairy brings me. Do you think it will be an action figure?"

"Silly, she's not Santa. She brings money. You know, a shiny quarter or something."

He yawned and stretched his arms over his head. "Maybe she'll bring an action figure because it's my first lost toof, and I took good care of it. Brushed it. Flossed. You know, I was a good kid."

She ruffled his hair. "Yes, you were and you are."

She kissed his forehead and switched on his nightlight. "Good night, little brother. Sweet dreams."

"Good night, big sis. I love you."

Warmth filled her. "I love you."

As she closed his door, she sighed.

Funny how words can change everything about how a person feels.

She entered the room she shared with Rachel to start her homework. Spread across the top of the comforter, feet kicking through the air as she read a teen magazine, Rachel resembled a model for an acne cream commercial. "I think Clinton Harris is hot."

Casey glanced at the glossy photo. Flippy hair, bright eyes, and glistening teeth. *Too young to be anything but cute.* "Is he a good actor?"

Rachel laughed. "He's a singer, silly. Here, listen." A pre-pubescent voice proclaimed undying love for his listeners.

No variation in tone. Juvenile lyrics. Still, she adores it. "Nice. I have to get my work done though."

The binding of "Intro to World Religions," groaned as it fell open. "Religion presents a way to make sense of living and dying. It lends higher meaning to the everyday experience." She rubbed her eyes and flipped a page.

"Every nation finds a way to mourn and honor their departed. Some cultures feel without proper demonstrations of grief, the spirit of the deceased cannot pass to the next realm." She skimmed ahead. "Professional mourners. Harbingers of death." *Sounds cheerful.*

Dad's car rattled in the driveway. Casey marked her place and skipped down the back stairs to greet him, Rachel running behind.

"Daddy!" The girls threw their arms around him. He smelled of gasoline and cologne.

He patted their backs and strained to peer around the corner into the living room. "How's Mom today?"

Rachel dropped the hug, a pout on her lips. "Bad. She didn't get off the couch at all again today."

Casey asked, "Hungry?"

As Dad walked to the living room, he answered, "Sure."

Casey jabbed her crestfallen sister in the ribs with her finger. "Want to help?"

"Not really."

"Ah, come on. I'll toast the cheese, and you heat the soup."

They set the plate on the kitchen table. Rachel called, "Dinner, Dad," then ran up the back stairs. Casey glanced in the living room. Mom clung to Dad's neck, and he slumped at an odd angle.

Her tears drenched his shoulder.

Casey whispered, "Dinner's ready, Dad."

He held up a finger.

She nodded and backed into the kitchen to wait. *Great, Ms. Melodrama has made an appearance. Never know with Mom which personality'll show up.* She scowled and strained to listen. Muffled complaints. *Wonder if she'll tell him how much we wicked children vex her?*

By the time Dad joined her, the soup required reheating. Casey poured the bowl into the saucepan. The gas stove would not ignite. Its click click click of gas release annoyed Casey.

Why can't Mom be normal? She grabbed a long-handled lighter and relit the stove's burner. It ignited with a burst. She stepped from the flames' heat.

By the time the soup warmed, her father had eaten the entire sandwich cold.

"I'm going to bed, Dad. It's been a long day. Do you have Malcolm's money?"

His creased forehead answered. "Malcolm's money?"

"Tooth fairy. Do you even have a quarter or something?"

"Geeze, Case, I forgot."

He searched his pockets. "I've got nothing." He dropped his head into his hands. "Maybe just give him a note that the tooth fairy will drop by tomorrow."

She glared. *I reminded him.* Heat rose in her face and roiled in her gut.

Malcolm will be disappointed.

Dark circles pooled under his eyes, and the fluorescent lighting accentuated the worry lines. Her heart plunged. *It's not his fault. He forgot.* She swallowed hard. "Right, Dad. Don't worry about it. I'll take care of it."

"Thanks, Case. You're a good kid." His head slid to the table, and he closed his eyes. *Twelve hour work days take a toll.*

Instead of returning to her school work, Casey scoured the house for money. *I can't even find loose change.* She peeked into the living room where her mother hugged a pillow and sobbed. *Not checking the cushions tonight.* Her stomach churned. *Shoot, what am I going to do? Malcolm doesn't deserve this disappointment.*

Her father's chest rose and sunk into a deep snore. *Guess we won't be talking about Kindergarten, either.*

She chewed her fingernails. *Nowhere else to look except the living room and that's not happening tonight.*

Eleven o'clock. End of shift for Aunt Hettie. She snatched the phone and dialed. "Hey, I'm sorry to bother you, but I need a favor. Could I borrow a dollar?"

"Sure. It was a good night for tips. What's going on?"

"Malcolm lost a tooth, and I don't have anything from the fairy."

"That's his first tooth, isn't it? Wow, that's a big deal! Maybe I should stop at the superstore and pick up something special."

"Nah, Aunt Hettie, just a bit of money is fine. I can't find anything here, and I don't want him to be disappointed."

"I'll be right over. How was your first day of school?"

"Good. I have a lot of homework already."

She chuckled. "Those walking the hallowed halls of academia do give lots of homework. Did you meet any cute guys?"

"Gosh, you're as bad as Rachel!"

"Ha-ha! I'll see you in a couple."

Casey's insides boiled. *I swear, if I didn't take care of things around here, the whole place would fall apart.* She slammed her book bag onto her bed and separated the folders and texts into subjects. *When did I become a mother?*

Her hands shook as she opened her first text book. The words blurred as tears trickled over her flaming cheeks. *It's so unfair. When did we lose our mother?*

She jotted notes, completed assignments, and read.

Casey greeted Aunt Hettie at the door with a grateful hug. "Shh, everyone's asleep."

"Look what I found." She pulled an action figure from a plastic shopping bag.

"Aunt Hettie, a quarter would have been fine." Her aunt's face crumpled. "He'll love it, though. Thanks!"

"Guess what else happened? It was a great day for tips, so I bought some groceries." She set three bags on the table. "Now tell me about school."

"I survived. I even made a friend, I think. Jaimie. She's a nice girl." *Talks a lot though.* "She's fun and smart. You'd like her."

Her eyes twinkled. "I bet I would."

"She asked me to go to a concert with her on Wednesday. I don't think I want to go."

Aunt Hettie slapped her hand on the table. "Why not?"

Casey jumped with surprise. *Why not?* Casey snorted. *Let's see. It'll be crowded there, and I don't want to be stuffed into a building with a bunch of people.*

She rubbed the back of her neck. *I won't know anyone except Jaimie, and what if I say something stupid and Jaimie doesn't want to be friends anymore? She might just leave me there, alone.* Sweat prickled along her hairline. *What if I can't breathe and pass out and people don't notice and step on me and crush me to death like I was some insignificant bug or something?*

She pictured ticking her complaints on her fingers before her aunt's astonished eyes. *She'd think I was nuts, like my mother.* Casey chewed her lip. *Gosh, what's wrong with me? I can't tell her all of this.*

Casey shrugged. "I don't want to leave the kids alone with Mom too long. Besides, I don't have the money."

Aunt Hettie studied Casey's face while she drummed her fingers. Casey squirmed under the scrutiny. "You know, I work mornings on Wednesdays. Could I pop over after work and make dinner? I don't get to see Malcolm and Rachel enough, in any case, and they are getting all grown up without me seeing it."

That's not true. Aunt Hettie visits all the time.

"Besides, it was a good day for tips today, and I want you to have a 'happy first day of college' present." She reached into her waitressing apron and pulled out some bills. "For you."

Casey swallowed a lump of gratitude. "I can't, Aunt Hettie. Thanks, though."

"Sure, you can, and I insist. Go to the concert, you crazy kid." She ruffled Casey's hair like she did when Casey was younger. "Take some time for yourself and try to enjoy school. There's lots to learn at college, and," she wiggled her eyebrows, "not all of it is found in the school books." Aunt Hettie covered a yawn with the back of her hand. "Promise me you'll tell me all about it?"

"About what?"

She set a handful of crumpled bills on the table. "The concert, of course."

"Aunt Hettie, I can't..."

Aunt Hettie cut off her protests with a hug. "Nonsense. Don't make your Auntie angry. I want you to live this life. You work so hard, and you deserve a break. Lots of breaks. You've been a grown up for too long, sweetheart." She held Casey by the shoulders and smiled. Spidery lines radiated from the corners of Aunt Hettie's weary eyes, badges of her hard work and kindness. She stood, leaving the money. "I'd better get going. I love you, kid."

Tears slicked her cheeks as her aunt's beat-up car pull away. *I have a great aunt!* Warmth spread through her as she locked the door once her aunt drove from sight.

Chapter Six

It's A Date

Malcolm zoomed around the house with his new action figure. A heroic grin lit his face. "Told you toof fairy'd bring me something special!"

Casey said, "You're right. Now get your shoes on, please." She checked on Mom. "Do you need anything?"

From her recline on the couch, Mom struggled to her elbow and snapped. "Why are you leaving again?"

"Work, Mom. School's Monday, Wednesday, Thursday, and Friday. Work's on Tuesday, Saturday, and Sunday."

"Why are you taking the kids?" She groaned as she swung her legs from the couch and slid them into dingy slippers. She caught Malcolm by the arm and pressed his cheek to her side.

"I'm taking the kids so that you can sleep." She pressed her lips tight. *Lies. Truth is to keep them away from your temper. Never know what you're going to do, now do we, Mom?*

"What if I need something while you're gone?"

Most kids rely on their moms to care for them. How did our lives get so turned around?

She studied her mother's face and searched for the familiar signs. Wrinkling at the corners of her eyes meant happy Mom might put in an appearance. She laughed and bestowed hugs and encouragement. No wrinkles. Lines snaking toward her tight-pressed lips indicated potential violence and trouble.

Doughy compliance.

This Mom wallowed in darkness and complained of abandonment. This Mom made Casey's blood run races through too-narrow veins. *You're supposed to take care of us, not tattle about our ingratitude to Daddy when he drags himself home from a double shift at one of his two jobs.*

Casey struggled to keep her voice steady. "You've got snacks and drinks on the side table. The remote is there. Your soaps are on TV. You should be set. Enjoy a quiet, relaxing day, okay?"

"But what if I need medical attention?"

"Mom, you'll be fine."

Malcolm wriggled in her hug. "Mom, you're strangling me." He burst from her grip and scampered out the door with a wave and a blown kiss. Rachel waved and dashed for the driveway.

"We'll be back before dinner time. I'll make spaghetti, okay?" Anticipating Mom's whining reply, Casey bustled the kids out of the house and into the car.

With their house a reflection in the rear-view, she said, "Remember, you have to be quiet at the library. I packed snacks. You can read or play with the computers, but you must behave."

Rachel crossed her arms and stared out the passenger window. Malcolm kicked his feet and played with his action figure. When they arrived, Casey situated them in the kids' area. She left Rachel with a satchel of snacks, coloring items, and quiet games. "I'll be manning the returns desk today if you need me, okay?"

Rachel tossed her head. "Whatever. Have a blast."

Casey took her post behind the return desk. She restocked and catalogued books, cleaned, and set up displays. She enjoyed the quiet of her work. One time, Aunt Hettie asked, "You're shy and you work all by yourself. Don't you get lonely?"

How can I be lonely when I'm surrounded by my best friends? Casey caressed a worn leather cover before restocking the book, *Jane Eyre*. One of her favorites.

She checked in on her siblings several times throughout the day, but they got on well. They played with the wooden train set, rearranging the pastoral scene to Malcolm's specifications.

They built fanciful block towers and drew pictures with crayons.

On her lunch break, Casey engaged them in games of Backgammon which she let them win. Rachel declared herself the overall champion. Casey and Malcolm congratulated her with dignified solemnity while Rachel lorded with hand waves and her nose pointed in the air.

Casey re-shelved the shambling pile of books her siblings had read, mostly picture books and kids' comics about superheroes. She returned to the circulation desk. While preparing a cart of donated items, she spotted the Kindergarten teacher and elementary principal talking in periodicals.

Thank you, God!

"Hi, Mrs. Hemshaw, Mrs. Nunzo." She nodded to the ladies. "I'm sorry to interrupt, but I have a situation."

Their brows raised with interest.

Casey gulped. *Shoot, how do I explain this?* Her gaze darted to her feet and the familiar quivery stomach announced anxiety. Her voice shook, but she forced the words. "Remember my little brother, Malcolm? I brought him in for Kindergarten registration."

Both nodded.

"Well, our Mom unenrolled him, thinking he's too young. He's not too young, right?"

"Not at all," Mrs. Nunzo said.

Casey bit her lower lip hard enough to draw blood, afraid to say something that would cause trouble. "Um, is there a way he can start this year?"

Mrs. Nunzo's brow crinkled, and she stood straighter. "Has your mother changed her mind?"

Sweat trickled through Casey's hair.

This morning, Dad said he knew Malcolm should start school, that he'd "talk sense" into Mom. "Well, my Dad's trying to convince her, and Malcolm really wants to start. He had such a nice time at the orientation."

Mrs. Hemshaw beamed. "It was delightful meeting him. Is he here?"

"Yes, in the Children's section, actually." Casey pointed.

Malcolm made little action figures walk through structures he'd created at the block table.

"He has quite an imagination, doesn't he?" The teacher walked over and bent to talk.

Malcolm's shy smile turned to a grin as he explained the castle he'd been building.

The principal placed a hand on Casey's arm.

Casey flinched, but did not pull away.

"I have his paperwork. Ask your Mom or Dad give me a call. I think Malcolm will start this year."

Casey thanked the principal. She visited the children's area and watched Malcolm and his would-be teacher interact.

Malcolm giggled as he turned the pages of a comic. He pointed to a photo of a spectacled older man on the back cover. "This is by Stan Lee." His eyes widened, and he bounced with enthusiasm. "He makes my favorite superheroes."

The teacher asked, "Do you know how to read any of these words?"

"Uh huh." He pointed to several and read.

The teacher clapped. "Very good. How did you learn to read so well?"

"My sisters taught me." He puffed out his chest.

Casey covered her mouth with a trembling hand. Tears glossed her eyes as she punched out at the end of her shift. She waved goodbye to her coworker and gathered up her siblings.

In the car on the way home, they sang loud choruses of Rachel's favorite Clinton Harris song "to get their sillies out."

Casey enlisted their help with dinner preparation. Malcolm opened a bag of frozen meatballs. Rachel broke spaghetti in half and poured jars of tomato sauce into a saucepan. Casey cooked.

They ate, cleaned up, and started another round of bedtime rituals.

As she tucked Malcolm into bed, he grabbed her hand. He guided it to his mouth. "Feel this."

"Ewe, no."

"Come on, Casey. I think I have another toof that can come out. Wiggle it."

"No. If it is loose, it will come out when the time is right."

He pawed his mouth. "But I want another action figure."

"First of all, that was a special something from the tooth fairy because you lost your very first tooth. However, a typical exchange involves a coin for a tooth. No action figures."

Malcolm smirked, tight-lipped and assured. "Uh huh. That's what you said about the other toof, but that fairy brought a present." He held up his toy and wiggled it before her. "I'm finking you aren't so smart."

I'm with you there, kiddo. "Well, I might not always be right, but I don't want you to be disappointed. I am pretty sure a normal tooth earns a coin. Maybe even a dollar." She ruffled his silky-fine hair. "Besides, you can't be yanking out teeth just to get presents. That's cheating." She tickled his belly, kissed his cheek, and turned out the light. "Say your prayers and get some sleep. I have school in the morning, and I may be late coming home tomorrow night."

"Why?"

"I was invited to a concert, and I might go."

"Can I come?"

"No, you have to be a grown up to attend."

"Then how can you go? You're just a kid."

Everyone needs to grow up sometime. "Good night." She closed the door and returned to her bedroom. The pile of school books waited for her attention.

The idea of school left Casey wide-eyed and nauseated.

What if Jaimie isn't there? What if I get lost or fail a class? I can't really afford college, and there is no guarantee I'll get a job in my field even if I do well in school. This could all be a huge waste of resources.

Her phone jingled a reminder. Casey read the text message Jaimie sent earlier in the evening:

Are we still on for the show?

She thought of the cash and advice Aunt Hettie gave. *More to learn than just what's in books.* She took a deep breath.

Yeah, I guess it's a date.

Chapter Seven

Musically Inclined

Bass pounded concussive blasts of metal music into the crowded, dark club. Casey's pulse responded to the beats, and her temples throbbed. She pressed her back against the black-painted wall. Percussion vibrated the wooden panel.

Jaimie danced. Her wiggling garnered appreciative glances from the crowd. Between songs, she leaned close and shouted, "They're great! I'm so glad you came with me!" before she returned to the dance floor.

Casey wavered a smile.

God, please get me out of here alive.

When people surged close, she edged away. Her eyes watered from overpowering perfumes and failed deodorants.

Hard to do circular breathing when you don't want to inhale.

A woman in a black cat suit took the microphone and screamed incomprehensible words.

Ryan played electric bass. Unbound, his hair reached his studded black leather belt. The drummer studied the singer and beat his kit without glancing at it.

Bet the keyboardist is underage. He doesn't look old enough to be out of high school. His cupid-bow lips pressed with determined delight.

Rachel'd think he was cute, I bet.

The lights died and plunged the venue into darkness. The crowd roared. Casey gripped the wall. *About 15 steps to the left, and I'm out the fire door.*

She shuddered. *If I pass out, though, this crowd'll pierce me with their spiked heels, and I'll be dead.*

A spotlight burned her eyes as it lit the guitarist who strumming a sad, acoustic song.

Jaimie swayed to the beat, arms up-stretched like a mermaid cutting a graceful progress to the surface of a pool.

Casey's ears rung in the relative quiet. Sweat trickled paths between her shoulder blades. *Surely this show is almost over.*

Jaimie yelled, "The guitarist's pretty cute, too." She bumped Casey with her hip, a playful smile on her lips.

Casey shook her head and stretched a hesitant smile. "You're as boy-crazy as my kid sister."

Casey stiffened when Jaimie hugged her. "You know, that's the first time you shared anything about your family. I call this progress."

Huh? Maybe it is progress at that.

Lights and pyrotechnics punctuated a blaring finale. The audience screamed their appreciation as the last whine of the guitar died away.

Casey's ears rang.

"Do you mind if we wait here?" Jaimie asked. "I want to tell Ryan what a great job they did." She hopped on the balls of her feet, searching backstage.

There's more air now with fewer people in the room.

While Jaimie applied lip gloss and kept a watchful eye for Ryan, Casey texted Aunt Hettie. "Is everything okay at home?"

The immediate response, "Yes, everyone's fine. Have fun." Casey breathed easier. She thumped her head against the wall and sighed. *Fun. Aunt Hettie's so optimistic. I survived.* When she swiped her hand across her forehead, she found it drenched. *Gosh, I hate crowds.*

Ryan's smooth voice caught her attention. "You came. Thanks, gals. What'd you think?"

Jaimie flipped her hair over her shoulder. "We loved it, didn't we Casey?"

Casey's mouth fell open. "Um, you have talent."

Ryan clapped a hand on her shoulder. "Not your cuppa tea, is it, Love? What do you normally listen to?"

"Mozart."

His eyes sparkled. "Yeah, we're a little more classic metal and a little less classical."

Casey stared at his steel-tipped boots. "Sorry."

"Hey, it's all good. You're honest and you came. Even if it was throwing you into the deep end without a warning." Kindness radiated from gentle eyes.

A shy smile crossed Casey's lips. *I can see why Jaimie's infatuated.*

He threw an arm around both girls' shoulders. Musky and masculine, he pulled them to his thin chest. "Are you two busy? We're heading to the soda shop. You should come."

Jaimie's reddened face and sharp intake of breath spoke of her desire. "What do you say, Case?"

When I texted, Aunt Hettie said everything's okay at home. Jaimie's fun, and Ryan seems nice. She shrugged. "I'd enjoy a good malted."

Ryan patted their backs. Casey winced, but not from the force. *Nobody usually touches me, except my family.* "Great. Meet you two there."

Once he disappeared backstage, Jaimie grasped Casey's hands. "Oh my gosh! This is amazing! I talked with him all summer, but he never asked me to join him. You are the best friend and my good luck charm."

She looked at Jamie's shaking hands. "Don't think anyone's ever called me either of those things before."

"Their loss, my gain." She kissed Casey's cheek.

Casey stiffened.

A cool breeze caressed their faces as they walked to the Bud's Soda Shop. Red and white checkers covered the tables and decorated the tiles. The air smelled of sweet cream and vanilla. Old-time crooners serenaded from a jukebox.

A sign advertised, "A quarter a tune. Five selections for a dollar."

"It's cute here. Don't think it's changed since my Uncle Carl attended though, and that was like in the 1950's." Jaimie chewed the gloss from her lower lip. "How many chairs do you think we need?"

Casey shrugged. "Beats me." The high-pitched ringing in her ears continued unabated. *I wonder if I'll suffer permanent tinnitus.* "It is cute here. Retro."

"It's not too busy yet, but I think most of our classmates are at Hemingway's Bar." She waved to a waiter Casey recognized as a student in her Calculus class.

"Can I push these tables together?"

He nodded. "Sure."

"Thanks."

The fake leather upholstery squeaked as they sat. The waiter brought menus.

"We'll wait to order until the others get here, but could we have two waters with lemon wedges? Thanks."

Jaimie tapped the tabletop, eyes on the door. "So, Casey, do you drink?"

"Alcohol? I'm underage."

Jaimie laughed. "So are most of our classmates, but that doesn't stop them."

"I don't drink alcohol."

"I didn't think so." Jaimie smiled. "Where're you from? I'm from Kittaning. Ever heard of it?"

"I've heard of it. I grew up in Butler, but we moved here when I was thirteen."

"We were practically neighbors. What a small, strange world."

A brass bell above the door announced the arrival of the Stages of Grief band. Jaimie waved them over.

When Ryan sat beside Jaimie, her cheeks glowed. "Thanks for getting us seats, girls."

He tipped his head to Casey. "Everyone, this is Jaimie, and this is Casey."

The band nodded greetings. Ryan pointed to the lead singer. "She's Red."

The auburn-haired beauty scowled a greeting and pushed the drummer into a seat.

"Knock it off, Rom, or I'll shove your drumstick somewhere you don't want it."

She plopped beside Casey arms and legs outstretched. Her deodorant needed refreshing.

Rom, the drummer, pulled a chair to squeeze beside Red. Casey shrunk into herself.

The guitarist motioned to the empty space beside Casey. "Do you mind?"

Casey shrugged. *Wish you wouldn't. Everyone's a bit too close at the moment.*

He sat. "Thanks." He loomed, oversized and muscular, beside her. His deodorant and cologne smelled nice.

Ryan sipped from Jaimie's water. "The axe man there is Tim, and our keyboardist," he pointed the striped straw at the youngest of their group, "is Tim's little brother, Tommy the Kid."

"Just Tommy." The boy balled up a napkin and threw it at Ryan. "I'm not that much younger than you."

The waiter took their order. Three baskets of fries and shakes all around.

Although Casey tried to shrink into obscurity, Tim insisted on including her in conversation.

He leaned close. She liked his cologne. Subtle and not fruity. "So, Casey, how do you like school so far?"

Casey blinked. "It's," she paused. "intense."

He nodded. "Can be. Want to try some of my shake? It's mocha madness, and it is good."

He pushed his frosty glass toward her.

"No, thanks." She sipped her malted. "I have my own."

He bit his lip as he smiled. "I noticed. Thought you might want to try something else."

Lumps of vanilla ice cream floated like icebergs in a milky sea. "No, thank you."

When not at school, Tim lived in a plan near the campus with Tommy and their family.

"You're practically neighbors," Jaimie said.

Tommy's face brightened, and his pert lips spread over perfect teeth. "Did you go to Ridge High?"

Rachel'd definitely think he was cute.

Casey nodded.

"You graduated last year? I graduate next year. I wonder why we never met while you were in high school."

Casey squirmed and played with some spilled sugar on the linoleum tabletop. The grit caressed her fingertips.

Probably because I'm usually invisible. "Not sure. It's not a big school."

"Nope." The young boy nudged his brother's elbow. "Tim-Tim, Casey's from around here, too. Did you meet her when you were in school?"

Tim pulled down a pair of aviator sunglasses and scanned her. His dark eyes looked as yummy as melted chocolate. "I heard. You went to Ridge? No way." He cocked his head, and heat rose in her cheeks, a slow and embarrassing progress. "Can't believe we never met." His eyes swept Casey. "I'd remember you."

The brothers' stares followed her every move the rest of the evening, making Casey's face burn. *Don't want to drink my malted. I'll probably slop all over myself.* So she took little, self-conscious sips.

The band told Casey and Jaimie how, Stages of Grief, formed. "It's all Tim's fault," Ryan said.

Tim leaned back and studied the ceiling. "Sure, blame me."

Ryan threw a fry. It hit Tim's chest and left a smudge of grease.

Tim pulled his brother into a headlock. "We had the idea together, actually. This little guy and me."

Tommy pushed free and pointed to Red. "She sang in the church choir when I was little, so we knew she had a good voice."

Red teased, "You still are little, squirt."

"Not too little. Bet I can even outplay Jon Lord." Tommy rubbed the dark stubble on his chin. "Just didn't know Red could belt out a tune better than Doro Pesch. Right, Tim?"

"That's not hard, though. Red's better than any of those poser chicks," Rom said. He wrapped his hairy arm around her neck, a human boa.

She pushed his hand away. "Thanks, but Doro's not a poser. She rocked."

Tim said, "Wonder what she's doing these days?"

"Living the life in Germany, no doubt." Red laughed.

Rom snorted. "Probably has like ten kids and weighs a couple hundred pounds."

"Don't dis the Doro." Red threw a fry. Rom tried to catch it with his mouth, but it bounced off his chin. "I'm telling you, the woman's bad-ass."

"What about Helloween? They knew how to rock," Tommy said. "They were from Germany, too, weren't they?"

"You know kid," Rom said, "Maiden's much better."

Tommy tapped his fingers along the tabletop. "Yeah, but see, we were talking about German bands, right? Besides, all those guys are ancient.

"Some don't even play anymore. What do you think of Imagine Dragons?"

Casey tuned out their descriptions of the musical merits of successful bands.

This is nice, just hanging with kids my age. Nobody demanding anything. Responsible for me alone. Her heart rate increased, and worry's heavy mantle descended.

Wonder how Rachel and Malcolm are holding up at home? She sent a covert text to Aunt Hettie. "Everything still good?"

Tim leaned across the table and spilled a container of fries. "Texting your lover?"

Casey slid the phone into her pocket, guilty as a shoplifter. Heat pained her flamed cheeks. "Uh, no."

The table fell silent an awkward moment. Jaimie's musical laugh burst forth. "Nah, she's letting Yngvei Malmstein know 'Stages of Grief' has a better guitarist than him."

Everyone except Casey chuckled. *Who's that?*

"Besides," Jaimie continued, a mischievous light in her eyes, "what would you care who she's texting?" She raised her eyebrows. "Unless you wish she were texting you."

Tim's smile answered as effectively as his words. "Well, I'd think that was pretty darned great." He held out his phone.

"What do you say? Hit me up with your digits?"

Rom pushed back to rest his boots on the table, arms cradling his head. "I think Tim-Tim's in love." A wolfish smile rested below lecherous eyebrows.

Oh My gosh, I wish I could melt as easily as this ice cream. I'd blend in with the floor tiles.

Tim studied her reaction and her obvious discomfort. "Shut up, Rom." He slid his phone into his pocket.

Red pushed Rom's feet off the table. "Yeah, shut up."

While Rom protested, Tim leaned closer and whispered to Casey, "Sorry. Didn't mean to embarrass you."

Casey shrank from his outstretched fingertips. *Bet he's warm and strong, and he sure seems nice.* She mumbled, "No big deal." But it was.

Ryan leaned in, a conspirator with big news. "Hey, everyone, listen. You're not going to believe it, but I got an invitation to that Equinox Ceremony."

"No way." Jaimie bounced with excitement.

Equinox Ceremony?

"Yeah," Ryan continued. "I met one of Dr. K's old students at a New Age bookstore in town. She helps run the thing. Only invites a couple of people, so it's pretty exclusive.

"She said to tell you about it. So, what do you say? Do you crazies want to join in the fun?"

"Of course!" Jaimie said, but something lurked in Jaimie's expression. A widening of her eyes. A flash of her nostrils.

What was it? Confusion? Fear?

Ryan explained, "The Enlightened Mind only allows seven participants. With you two, we're seven. So you gotta come."

"But what do they do?" Tim asked. His gaze darted between his brother and Casey.

Red leaned in, all wild eyes and wilder hair. "They explore the mystical. Being included is a huge honor."

Jaimie all but leapt into Ryan's lap. "I'm there. You can count on me."

Ryan gave her a hug. Jaimie squealed. "That's great." He tilted his head toward Casey. "What about you?"

All eyes bored into her. *If I don't go, they're one short.* She bit her lip and whispered, "I guess I can come."

Jaimie clapped. Tim leaned into his chair, quiet. Tommy punched the air. Ryan raised his milkshake. "To the Equinox, then, and all the secrets it will reveal."

Casey joined the others in the toast. *Wonder why Tim looks worried?*

After disconcerting slaps on the back and a hug from Jaimie the group dispersed.

Students traveled in small, noisy packs between restaurants, bars, and dorms.

Deep lung-full of the cool night air calmed her as she made her way to her car.

What have I gotten myself into?

A deep voice and running footfalls interrupted her thoughts. "Casey, wait up." Tim jogged to her side. "You shouldn't walk to your car alone."

Casey calmed her heartbeats to keep time with her falling feet.

"You don't mind, do you? I walk Tommy, too, so it's not a sexist thing."

"Where is Tommy?"

Tim stumbled. "He's waiting for me." He thrust his hands into his pockets. "Yeah, so maybe it's a bit of an old-fashioned gentleman thing. But I did want to tell you I'm really glad you came tonight. I liked meeting you and hope I see a lot more of you."

Casey unlocked her car, grateful for the dark disguising her burning face. "It was nice meeting you too." She lingered an eternal second. "Well, bye." She slid into the car and started the engine.

Tim knocked on the window. "Bye, Casey. Drive safely."

All the way home, Casey's ears rang with music, chatter, and the hope of new friendships. *That was fun.* She hummed one of the Stages of Grief songs, an Ozzy Osbourne cover she'd never heard before.

Tim's words, "hope I see a lot more of you," threaded through her excitement.

At home, everyone slept when Casey tiptoed to her bed. Rachel had left a folded sheet of paper on her pillow. Inside, she and Malcolm had written, "Good night, Casey. We love you."

Casey snuck a peek at the kids and pulled their covers over their shoulders. "I love you, too." She kissed their sleeping heads.

Chapter Eight

New Plans

I can't believe I agreed to this.

Casey trudged up the hill overlooking campus. Her thigh muscles complained when she paused. *From this perspective, NorEast looks like a miniature village under a Christmas tree.* Stone passageways meandered through the buildings. Smoke from the brewery billowed as though creating the fluffy clouds that drifted through the darkening sky.

Casey remembered the trepidation of her first weeks of school. *Now, I know those buildings. I belong.*

Jaimie waited, so she returned to her trek. Autumn lent a tang to the air. Casey's pace slowed with misgiving.

Jaimie called from further up the path. "Stop dawdling, Casey. We're going to be late. Gosh, it took you forever to get here. The band's there already."

"I came as soon as I was done with work."

Jaimie pressed her lips together. "You work too much."

"Some of us have to pay for our own schooling."

"Hey, I took out my own loans to be here. I'm amassing a debt in the name of education, thank you very much."

Fog rolled in, muffling and obscuring sound.

Weird. I thought fog settled lower. Wonder why it's up here, but there's none in the campus valley?

The trees grew closer and blocked the failing September sunshine. *It will be dark soon.* She patted her pocket where her flashlight rested. Primordial discomfort made Casey cast hurried glances into the shadows. *Wonder what's watching us from the shady edges?* She hurried to catch her friend.

Jaimie grabbed her hand and pulled her along.

Casey shivered. *Wish I'd brought a sweater.*

Jaimie tilted her head. "Are you feeling okay?"

"Yeah, why?"

"It's kind of hot, but you have gooseflesh." She giggled. "You're not creeped out, are you?"

Fog engulfed their ankles, twisting like the fingers of the damned.

"Oh, come on! This is going to be fun. I'm so excited! I can't believe we were included in the Autumn Equinox ceremony."

Casey gulped. *Me, either. How did we warrant an invitation? Ryan barely knows me.*

"How cool that Dr. Krochalis just covered seasonal rites. Makes me feel we might know what's going on. Everyone says the experience is amazing."

Casey had shivered. *So you all keep saying.*

Jaimie squeezed her hand and whispered. "We're here." A bonfire roared in a small clearing in the deciduous trees and sent sandalwood sparks toward the dimmed sky. A stand of shorter pines resembled sentinels at the ready. The bandmates shuffled their feet, hands in pockets beneath the trees' massive shadows. Three older people huddled near a fallen tree trunk, their heads together in conspiratorial conference.

Ryan detached from the group and rushed to embrace the girls. Jaimie clung to his waist.

Jaimie, you're so obvious with your crush. Come on, girl. If he's not going to pay attention, there are plenty of guys who are interested. Ryan detached and escorted them to the rest of the group. He whispered, "I worried you'd be late."

A shared, mild electricity animated them, except the elders who continued their discussion. Tommy swayed like a tree in a breeze. Rom made swipes for Red's hand, but she skittered away.

Tim smiled. "Hello." The constant shifting of his eyes betrayed unease. "You look like a ray of sunshine."

Casey blushed at his compliment.

Jaimie insisted Tim would be asking Casey out any day now. *He hasn't asked thus far, now has he?*

Besides, Jaimie also anticipated dating Ryan. *I don't see him asking her out, either, though.*

Her friend twirled her hair and giggled, all feminine sighs and batting lashes. Ryan ignored her attempts to attract his attention. Instead he studied the fire and fidgeted.

Casey shook her head.

One of the organizers spread her arms as though in welcome and cleared her throat. She waved a hand as though moving it through water. "Come, gather around. I am Lily, and this is Mabon." She indicated a plump man in his thirties. She glided to a tree stump where a statuesque woman held out cloaks. Lily and the woman donned long red cloaks, and Mabon slipped on a dark robe.

After a glance at the sun, Lily announced. "It's time to begin."

Chapter Nine

Serpent's Stare

Dusk descended as a veil whose darkest folds hid multitudes of watchful eyes. Lily lit herbs in an abalone shell and fanned the smoke over them. Casey felt light-headed and coughed. "What is that?"

Lily flapped a feather spray, directing the smoke billowing from a conch shell. "Herbs. This ceremony is all about balance. The shell is from the sea, feathers the air, herbs the earth, and fire is its own element." Red embers quickly devoured a dried sage leaf.

Casey wrinkled her nose. "What kind of herbs, though? I see sage, right?"

Jaimie tugged her hand. She whispered, "Who cares? They're herbs." Her narrowed eyes and taut muscles seethed agitation.

Casey recoiled. "I'm just curious."

Jaimie continued with terse whispers, "You know, you pick a heck of a time to suddenly become communicative, Ms. Usually Taciturn. This is a sacred space."

Dirt underfoot. Trees shedding leaves. Ill-mannered bonfire consuming tree skeletons, popping and spreading sparks.

Not like any church I've ever visited. Casey blinked back tears. The herbs stung, but so did Jaimie's disregard for her concerns. *You don't want to be kicked out. Ryan wants to be here, and you want to be with Ryan.*

Tim closed the gap and whispered, "I'm glad you're asking. I wondered the same thing." He tugged at his jacket collar, glances darting. Casey gravitated toward him and hovered near his solid and somehow familiar form. *He reminds me of my dad a little.* His nearness comforted, like a watchful family dog ready to defend against intruders.

Mabon's cold hands on her shoulder made Casey jump. His rich baritone tickled her ear. "We're here to teach. You'll understand soon."

She shivered.

Tim edged closer, eyes narrowed, jaw clenched.

Don't like this Mabon character. He's creepy, and I think he's looking down my top. She ducked her chin, sending her hair to cover cleavage revealed from his greater height. She sidled away from Mabon and stood closer to Tim, a sentry on alert.

Mabon moved on to massage Jaimie's shoulders.

A glance told the truth. *Yep, he's looking down her top now.*

Casey's stomach complained, and her head hurt.

I should go home, but look at them.

Her friends twittered with anxious enthusiasm as Lily brushed herbal smoke over them. "This is the smudge ceremony. Ancient ritual observed by the tribes in this area. Can any of you claim Native blood?"

Red raised a shaking hand. "I have Cherokee ancestors."

Huh? Red's nickname came from her auburn hair and freckles. I'd not peg her as Native American.

Rom snaked an arm around Red's waist. "My pretty squaw."

She pushed away and snarled, "Get off."

Mabon shook his head. "Squaw is an insult. Women should not be reduced to a single body part. That's what the word means. A woman's private bits."

"Ewe, Rom, you dick! What's wrong with you?" Red punched his arm.

Casey hid her amused giggle behind a contrived cough. *Ironic much?*

Rom waved his hands warding off her anger. "I-I didn't know. I thought squaw meant woman. You know, like in the old Westerns."

Lily said in a breathy voice, "This is no place for discord. It is an assembly of unity." She extended her hand and glided to the angered couple. The firelight made her golden curls and milky skin glow.

She set a hand on each of their shoulders. "We among the rainbow tribe harbor many misconceptions."

I'd guess she's Nordic. How's she know about Native American culture? What are her credentials?

As though he read her thoughts, Mabon said, "The rainbow tribe is what the Native People call non-native people. We all have common ancestors, after all, and our tribes have diverse colors."

Nervous energy emboldened Casey. "So, is this an Indian ritual?"

Lily pointed at her. Her voice sounded shrill as a territorial jaybird. "See, that's what I'm talking about. Indian is a hurtful name bestowed on the tribes by Columbus."

Mabon spit on the ground. "Columbus was a twit."

Lily bent to study Casey's face. "Wait, have we met before?"

Casey shrunk into herself, like a hermit crab disappearing into a shell. A weird thought popped into her mind. *The lily is a death flower.*

The other woman strolled to them. A gentle breeze accompanied her approach, caressing cheeks and pushing back hair. Its softness reminded Casey of a doting mother.

Not that my Mom's loving.

The fog swirled about her hem, a phantom ball gown swaying with her movements. Her voice calmed everyone. "None of this matters."

She also bent to lock eyes with Casey. Casey held her breath, a frozen rabbit caught in a serpent's stare. "This ritual is ancient, but it comes from all cultures. It has many names. What it will do for you, for you all, is reveal your true natures." She spread her arms, the robe dangling like the wings of a vast bird of prey.

Cassandra. Her name's Cassandra. I don't know why I know that, but I'm sure it's true.

Casey gulped. Her heart pounded.

Everyone joined hands and formed a circle around the fire. Tim's felt warm as it engulfed hers. Mabon and Lily patrolled the perimeter. Cassandra stood close to feed the flames with dried branches and bundled herbs. Heady smoke rose Heaven-ward. She intoned words Casey did not recognize. Lily and Mabon mimicked her. The band mates' mouths moved along.

"What are we supposed to do?" Casey whispered. Tim shrugged and followed his brother's enthusiastic lead by lending his voice to the rising chant.

The woman threw amber powder into the air. It settled into their hair, pungent as curry spices. The scene quivered, like heat risen from the ground on a sweltering day. A wind circled and sent spirals of sparks and gem-bright leaves.

It penned them in. The air grew heavy, thick with riddles.

Murmured secrets rolled through the underbrush to infiltrate and buzz in Casey's head like an angry bee hive. Unseen chimes tinkled. Sweat cooled on her skin. Desperate, she held her breath.

The world swirled. She knees crumbled and scraped her cheek on rough bark. It lapped up her blood, leaving no trace of her presence. From every direction, golden eyes growled, bristling fur howled, and silver scales swam together to form a harvest moon.

The chanting swelled, a great storm-tossed ocean wave. Casey gasped, pressed against a weight compressing her chest. The words grew intelligible. She chanted with the others, and the squeezing relented.

"Equal day and equal night, balance in all things. What hid within to be revealed, the balance resets."

Chapter Ten

Off Her Meds

Casey's head rang and throbbed, and her stomach rejected thoughts of food. She woke atop her comforter. Her feet, still in dirty sneakers, dangled over the edge of the bed. Slight movements made her queasy. The world reeled. *How'd I get here?*

She smelled of bonfire and moldered leaves. *Ugh. I need to clean up.*

She leaned against the shower stall. The ground spun, her stomach heaved, and she threw up. Warm water cascaded over her in the shower. *It's like it passes right through me, like I'm no more substantial than a ghost.* She held her palms before her face and studied their lines. *Never noticed how different the left is from the right. There are nearly no lines on the left side. Wonder why.*

She dried, dressed, and listed downstairs to make breakfast. Coffee and bacon wafted. *Dad must be home. Don't have to cook after all.* Her stomach growled. *Wonder if I can eat, or if that's too heavy? My tummy's a bit touchy just now.*

Casey stepped into the kitchen and stumbled. *Couldn't be.* Her head throbbed. *What on earth? Mom hasn't cooked since she was pregnant with Malcolm.*

With a clatter of pans, her mother started another skillet. The sink overflowed with dirty dishes and cooking implements. Her siblings gobbled plates of scrambled eggs with melted cheese. Platters heaped with breakfast meats shared table space with a basket of biscuits and a plate of current scones. Rachel cut a slice of ham and cheese quiche. Casey tiptoed to her seat, confusion over last night replaced with concern about the here-and-now. *What's this mean?* She broke a piece of a crumbled scone and chewed.

Rachel pushed the butter dish and whispered, eyes wide and dark-rimmed in her pale face. "I hope you're hungry."

The laden table could provide food for at least a dozen hungry people. Casey said, "Mom, this looks great. What's the occasion?"

Her mother spun and wiped her hands on a stained apron. "I didn't know you were here." She scrutinized Casey and frowned. "You look like Hell. Are you hung-over?"

Sheesh, since she's always on the couch, I forgot how formidable she is. Casey shrunk into the seat as though the scant distance provided would be of help. She avoided eye contact. "No, Mom. You know I don't drink."

Mom narrowed her eyes, pinch-lipped with disbelief. "Why were you out so late?"

Memories of rhythmic drums accompanied the pounding in her brain. Fanciful images devoured by firelight sent to the skies in golden sparks haunted her imagination.

She shook her head and regretted the movement. She rested a hand on her temple. "School stuff. Research for comparative religions class."

Her mother scoffed. "What's there to compare? God is God. Religion is when we go to church. Sounds like a bogus class to me."

Casey shrugged and poured a cup of coffee and hoped to avoid scrutiny with activity.

She changed the subject. "Are we expecting guests?"

"What? Why would we be expecting guests?"

Grease dripped from a deep-fried hash brown and settled in a dark pool on the tablecloth.

Casey bit her lip and considered her tone. Slow, steady, and calm words hid her unease. "It's just this is a lot of food for us, don't you think?"

Mom's cheeks swelled, a volcano of emotion contained by a single passage.

Malcolm and Rachel hunkered in their chairs, leaving Casey to attract the lightning strike of Mom's fury.

Mom poked her finger into Casey's collar bone.

"What a judgmental thing to say, you ungrateful girl! You lie about in bed, hung-over from consorting with a bunch of college kids, acting like you're better than everyone else while I slave to create a nutritious meal."

She motioned to the feast. "Instead of appreciating my effort, you denigrate it. How dare you?" Spit sprayed and coated Casey. "You are excused until the others have eaten. Go to your room and think about your arrogance. When they are done, you can return to clean up this mess."

Each syllable struck like a hammer. Casey blinked hard but tears spilled over her flaming cheeks.

She ran to her room, grabbed her phone, and texted Dad at work. "I think Mom's off her meds."

I know I shouldn't bother him at work, but what am I supposed to do?

She paced to mitigate the anger, hurt, and confusion. *This is all too much.*

Her head buzzed like bees had taken residence. The racket pressed against her eyes, and she massaged her temples for relief.

She curled on her bed, pressed a pillow to her lips, and shouted until she grew hollowed of her anguish.

Chapter Eleven

A World in a Dream

Casey woke, no longer able to ignore the sunbeams dancing across her eyelids. She groaned and rolled over. Dangerous dreams haunted, but the headache diminished.

Not ready to face today, but I guess I'd better clean the kitchen before Mom flips her lid.

Clanking in the kitchen made her pause. *Shoot. Mom's going to kill me if it's her cleaning.* Casey crept to the doorframe and peeked. Rachel stood on a chair at the sink. Malcolm gathered dishes. *No Mom.* Casey breathed easier.

She tried to sound cheerful. "Hey, you two! Are you putting me out of a job?"

They paused and smiled. Casey gasped. Rachel wore the cares of an older woman. Dark-circled eyes puffed from lack of sleep and suppressed tears. Pale and haunted, she resembled a character from gothic literature. A bitter smile crossed Casey's face. *She looks like me.*

Casey ignored tears that prickled her eyes. With a dash, she crossed to grab her sister around the waist. She swung Rachel off the chair and kissed her cheeks.

She placed her sister's feet on the floor and smiled at both kids. "You little darlings. I'll clean this."

Rachel scowled at the mess. She shook her head. "It's too much. We'll help."

"Yeah." Malcolm dropped a plate to the floor. Pancakes bounced, rolled, and splatted. Crestfallen, he blushed and buried his chin into his collar, and sniffed. "Sorry."

Casey ruffled his hair and picked up the mess. "See, this helps put me in motion. How clever of you! Malcolm, can you please get the plastic wrap from the pantry?"

He brightened. "Sure."

She tapped her chin. *Think she used every pot and mixing bowl we own.* As she assessed how best to approach the cleanup, a question formed. She peeked into the living room.

"Hey, Rachel, where's Mom?"

Rachel shrugged. "I don't know. She went out."

"Out?" *Mom balked at leaving the living room.* "Where'd she go?"

"I don't know. She said she needed to pamper herself."

Could this be a good thing? Maybe Mom pulled out of her depression. But her stomach plunged. *Worry about it if something happens.*

She pulled her hair into a ponytail. "So kids, how's school going?"

Rachel launched into the latest elementary school drama while Malcolm bounced with enthusiasm. "I can read two of the beginner books. Want to see?"

Casey nodded, and he dashed to his room. He read aloud while the girls tidied.

After they finished cleaning, she said, "Thank you so much for your help. Like Gram used to say, 'many hands make light work.' You two are the best. Let's get some ice cream. My way of saying thanks."

Her phone chirped. A text message from Jaimie. "What are you doing?"

"Getting ice cream for my little brother and sister. Why?"

"Can you come get me? Please?"

"Are you okay?"

A pause, then, "Yeah. Are you coming?"

Casey turned to her siblings. "Hey guys, would you like to meet my friend Jaimie?" The kids bounced and clapped.

She texted, "On our way."

Chapter Twelve

We All Scream

Jaimie bolted through the parking lot as though pursued by a monster. She leaped in the passenger seat and locked the door. "Hi! I'm glad to meet you." She twisted to smile at the kids.

Malcolm pressed into the seat. Rachel cocked her head and leaned closer. "Hi." With a quizzical tilt to her eyebrows, she studied Jaimie.

Jaimie embraced Casey about the neck, then buckled her seatbelt. "Let's go." Her foot tapped, and she patted her thighs faster than the boy-band on the radio.

Casey pulled from the parking spot. Her stomach tossed, as though motion sick, but she said, "Let's go to the custard shop in Delton. Sound okay?"

"Sure," the kids answered.

Jaimie twitched like bugs crawled over her skin.

They reached the roadside stand with its cheerful white and blue striped awning. They walked through a patio crowded with circle tables and chairs beneath matching striped umbrellas. Only a few were occupied.

A clerk whose name tag read "Candy" bounced to the window. Her long ponytail peeked from beneath her blue striped cap. She wiped her hands on the matching apron front. "What can I get for you?"

Malcolm raised his hand. "My favorite is cotton candy explosion. Can I have that kind, pwease?"

Candy complied. Malcolm took a lick and opened wide. "Listen, my mouth is sparkling."

Jaimie tipped her head closer. "It is! Does that have Pop rocks or something in it?"

Candy's chirpy voice confirmed. "Yes, it does!"

Rachel pinched her lips and crossed her arms. "Close your mouth, Malcolm. Nobody needs to see your ice cream once it is inside you."

Malcolm stomped his foot. "You're not in charge, Miss Bossy Pants."

Casey ruffled his hair. "That's enough, you two. Malcolm, pick a table for us. Four chairs please." She smiled at Rachel. "What flavor do you want?"

Rachel frowned. "He gets away with everything."

"Rach," Casey ran a hand down her sister's long hair. "Don't worry so much. This is time to have fun." She chose from the long list of custom-made flavors. "I'll have a small caramel ribbon, please."

She turned to Rachel. "How about you?"

"Guess I'll have chocolate." She squinted at the sign and whispered, "Can I have sprinkles? It's twenty-five cents extra."

Casey nodded.

Candy asked, "Chocolate sprinkles or rainbow?"

"Rainbow, of course." Over Rachel's bed at home hung an inspirational poster. It featured a unicorn running over a rainbow. In sparkling letters, it read, "Never give up on your dreams."

Sure, hope she'll get everything she wants from life. She's a great kid.

"How about you, Jaimie?"

"Oh, I'll get my own," she said.

Should have enough, even if she orders a large.

Casey frowned. "You're my guest. Order something, please, and don't insult me."

Jaimie smiled. "I'll take the fish food. A small please," she told Candy. "Thank you, Casey."

They collected their treats and found the table Malcolm had chosen. Breezes buffeted their hair and burnished their cheeks crimson.

Jaimie bounced. Her cone dripped on the tabletop. Malcolm wrinkled his eyebrows. "Do you have to go potty?"

They laughed.

"No, I just can't sit still any more. Not since—"

Since the ceremony. Casey noted dark circles beneath her friend's eyes and worry creases where smooth skin stretched days before. *Were we drugged? Last night at the ceremony, was there something other than sweet-grass and sage in those smudge sticks?* Smokey images floated.

Wolves devoured lambs. Native Americans smoked pipes. Water and music took human form.

She reached a hesitant hand toward her friend. Her stomach lurched as though she stood aboard a ship tossed in a storm. *Not used to initiating touch. Jaimie hugs. I hug my kid sister and brother.* Her voice cracked. "Are you okay?"

Jaimie whispered, "I'm not sure." Her eyes widened and her lower lip quivered.

Casey's breathing became difficult, and her knees knocked as though she'd just run a 5K.

Jaimie's vulnerable, and I don't know what to do to help.

Casey's head ached, and she looked away. Tears threatened as Jaimie's emotion washed over her.

A couple at the nearest table fed a baby frozen delight. The baby's face crinkled to the cold. The mother's laughter sounded far away.

Traffic whizzed, heedless in their pursuits of home and errands.

A dark-haired boy flirted through the order window with Candy, and she pushed him aside when a family approached.

A man, a woman, and two children.

Cold washed over Casey. Numbed, she stared.

They dripped gore. Burned, blackened skin peeled from their faces. Their mouths formed grotesque, too-wide grins. Smoke rose from their charred flesh toward the autumn-gray sky.

Casey gasped as the father glared with death-clouded eyes. Her eyes bulged, yet she couldn't turn away. *Can barely breathe.* The mother pushed her children to the window. Blood-drenched hair shrunk around a hole in the little boy's head. *He's about Malcolm's age. The girl's a bit younger than Rachel.*

Casey covered her mouth to muffle an odd, muddled croak. The stench of charred skin and hair clung to her throat. She gagged.

Are they accident victims? Casey pushed from the table, ran to the trash bin, and threw up. She rested her forehead against the cool plastic liner, grateful the sugary garbage masked the char and blood.

Maybe I imagined it?

With a shudder, she lifted her head and stole a glance. The family whispered, huddled as Candy brought plastic spoons with samples.

The little boy clapped; skin fell to the pavement with a splat and splash of puss and blood.

Casey's stomach squeezed. *I don't understand. Why isn't anyone helping them?*

Their covert glances unnerved. Casey bit into her trembling lower lip. *It's too early for Halloween, and those are definitely not costumes.* She squinted to be sure. *Makeup can be pretty intense, but nobody seems to care that they're spilling blood everywhere.* She closed on them, fighting the desire to run away. *Not makeup. I can see the man's brain pulsing.* Gas fumes and char emanated from them.

Queasy again, a wave of lightheadedness accompanied the unreality. Tears drenched her shirt and hair.

The gore-encrusted family clutched sugar cones, and the father ushered them to their car.

Its red paint glinted like the blood sliding down the children's faces to saturate their clothes. The girl stared out the window at Casey.

Tears slid unhindered, slicking Casey's face. A cold little hand slid into hers. Rachel's quiet voice quavered with worry. "Are you okay?"

As the family pulled out of the parking spot to enter traffic, Casey trembled and wailed, "No."

Warm bodies pressed against her legs. Malcolm whispered, "What's wrong, Sis?"

Casey caressed his cheek, unable to stifle her weeping. *Maybe this is how Mom feels when she can't stop crying.*

Rachel squeezed her other hand. Her voice shook, "What happened? What's wrong?"

I can't explain. Violent quakes tore through her body and tears dammed within her throat until she couldn't make a sound. *I'm going crazy, I guess. But that poor family!* Casey cradled her head and rocked.

Brakes screeched and a metallic crunch dropped Casey to her knees. She pressed Rachel and Malcolm's heads to her shoulders.

Rachel screamed, "What's happening?"

Malcolm clung to his sisters and cried.

Casey kept their faces pinned and shielded from the accident.

Running, screams, and yelling confused everything. Black smoke billowed from the pile-up. Crunched between two sedans, the red car resembled a crushed Coke can. Casey quaked, as tears dripped into her siblings' hair.

Jaimie grabbed her phone. "Please send help. There's been an accident." Her voice pitched high, close to hysteria, as she described the scene.

A concussive explosion elicited screams from everyone.

Gas, burned plastic, and something worse.

Shattered glass splayed in a cloud of black smoke.

The crowd retreated. Some collapsed to the pavement. Others skittered around the emblazoned vehicle, unable to pull the bodies from the ruins.

Malcolm hugged Casey tighter.

Rachel pushed away. Stiff, upright, and with false bravado, she asked, "Do you think they're all right?"

Jaimie rested one hand on Rachel's shoulder and the other on Casey's. "People are helping, and an ambulance is on the way. I think I hear the siren." Tears slid unabated, gushing grief over Casey's face. She swallowed a response. *No, none of them will survive. Not sure why I know, but I do.*

An ambulance and police car wailed onto the scene. Chaotic lights added to the pandemonium. Uniformed officers jotted statements from witnesses. Paramedics loaded bodies onto gurneys.

Quick movements, practiced attention, and studied control, the hallmark of professional medical personnel. *They betrayed nothing.*

Peace settled over Casey. Her tears dried, and without knowing why, she didn't doubt—*They're already dead.*

Chapter Thirteen

Some Images Stay

Jaimie ran a shaky hand through her hair. Sprays like sun-kissed sea water washed over her shoulders. "Can I hang out with you for a little while? Please. I don't want to go back yet."

Casey's voice croaked. "I guess. I don't think I'll be good company, though." *I'm drained, cried out. Hollow. That poor family.* The girl's face as they pulled away haunted the space behind her eyelids. With every blink, the girl greeted Casey with varied levels of accusation and duress. Sometimes the girl's eye slid from its socket and hung by the optic nerve on her blackened cheek. Other times through singed hair and crushed features, she smiled and transformed into a whole, lovely child and waved with her brother and parents.

Why didn't I stop them from leaving? I think I knew what would happen.

The boy's ice cream had dripped over its cone onto the boy's hand. His mother had wiped the sticky sweets from her son.

Could I have stopped them?

The father had rushed his family from Casey retching into a garbage bin.

Did I cause them to crash? Maybe I freaked out the dad by throwing up into the garbage bin, and he didn't pay close enough attention to driving?

Casey struggled with guilt. She said nothing on the trip home. Rachel hummed along with pop songs on the radio. Malcolm stared out the window. Rural scenery gave way to their housing plan. The gravel grumbled as she pulled her car into the parking space and turned the engine off. She pressed deeper into the seat, reluctant to move.

Rachel cleared her throat and motioned to the wood-framed farmhouse. "Welcome to our home, Jaimie. We never have guests, so this is really cool."

Malcolm studied the lacing on his shoes. "Yeah. Guess what, Jaimie? I lost a toof. See?" He pointed to the vacancy in his mouth. "Toof fairy gave me an action figure. You want to see him?"

Jaimie chuckled. "Sure. As soon as your sister is ready, you can show it to me."

Rachel shuffled her feet. "Are we going inside, Case?"

Casey sighed. She allowed her eyes to close, but she jolted upright. The mangled car waited in the quiet behind her lids. Tears welled, and a lump burned in her throat.

Jaimie touched Casey's forearm, concern played across her features. She whispered, "What the heck is going on?"

Casey gasped for breath and fought a renewed onslaught of tears. She shook her head and breathed. "I wish I knew."

One of the kids whispered, "Let's go." They exited the car and held hands, waiting for the older girls to join them. When neither girl moved, the younger pair wandered through the yard. Standing close together in the sunlight. *Perfect angels.* Memories of the doomed children made her stomach convulse. *Why is life so short?* She sniffed back snot. *Tears again. I don't think I've ever cried so much in my life. Not that I haven't had reasons.*

Casey asked, "Did you see them?"

Jaimie's foot stopped its motion for a moment. "See who?"

"That family at the ice cream stand."

Jaimie sounded wary. "Do you mean the ones who crashed? I guess so. Why?"

I don't understand. Her lip trembled. *Am I going crazy?* "What did they look like?"

Color rose along Jaimie's jawline and infiltrated her cheeks. Her confused brow and shaking head made Casey gulp. Jaimie's voice sounded small, frightened. "What do you mean?"

"What did they look like? You know, anything unusual about their appearance?"

"No, I guess, they looked ordinary. You know, middle class, nice clothes, respectable. What are you looking for?" Jaimie leaned against the door, eyes distrustful, hand on the handle. "What did you see?"

Darn tears! I'm done with all this emotion.

"They looked—wrong. Bloody." She hiccupped on her tears.

Jaimie extended a shaky hand. "Maybe you had a vision? Like a premonition."

Casey covered her face and sobbed. "Well, if so, what good did it do? They still died."

She felt Jaimie's tentative embrace. Her kindness broke the final dam of Casey's stymied emotion. She shook and wailed until she heaved dry raspy breaths.

Sniffing, she pushed from Jaimie and stammered, "I'm sorry. I don't know what's wrong with me."

The haunted expression returned to Jaimie's eyes. "I don't know. I'm feeling off myself."

Casey touched her friend's hand. "Let's go inside and get some lemonade. We can talk there."

"Sounds good," she said, her words lackluster and flat.

I get that. Nothing sounds good to me, either, but let's make the best of things.

She called the kids, and the four stepped inside.

Rachel gasped. "What the heck?"

Malcolm's eyes bulged, and his mouth fell open.

Jaimie giggled.

Before them stood Casey's mother, not a single thread upon her body, hair tangled with autumn leaves. Milky folds of fat tumbled over her c-section scar, and her heavy breasts rested on her ample belly.

Casey screamed, covered her brother's eyes, and pushed her friend toward the door. Frantic, she yelled, "Oh my gosh, Mom, where are your clothes?"

Chapter Fourteen

Brain Honey

Casey's concentration waned, and lectures blended together. Interrupted sleep left her head buzz like bees nested between her ears.

Funny how everyone seems to be saying similar things. Universality. Jungianism. History recreates itself. What is in vogue, cycles. Trends repeat. Even Mathematics discusses statistical comparisons of sameness.

The drone reminded her of lazy summer afternoons before Malcolm's birth. Her family picnicked in the little park near Lackawanna Creek. She liked to spread the checkered blanket beneath shade trees and watch the insects scurry across the ground and fly overhead.

She sometimes drifted on the water in a rented inner tube, stretched beneath a cloudless sky while her parents cuddled Rachel close by on the rocky beach.

Casey's head bounced, and she jolted from the doze. *Shoot. Hope no one saw me.*

Jaimie's head rested on her folded forearms. A quiet snore escaped.

Casey nudged her friend and shushed her when she startled.

An Emo-clad student raised a black-finger-nail-painted hand. "Excuse me, but aren't we supposed to cover psychopomps in this class?"

Dr. Bridges' eyebrows raised above his spectacles. "Psychopomps? You mean messengers of death, those entrusted with the safe passage of a soul to its afterlife? Why no, that would be a matter to be discussed in a religion or mythology class. We study the human mind, and our studies are outlined on the clever syllabus I distributed on the first day of class." The student pulled her knitted hat low over her black-dyed hair. "Sorry."

Devon stood. "Wait, a minute. Aren't psychos crazy people? I mean, that's what psychology studies, right? Crazies?"

Dr. Bridges' expression darkened. "People afflicted with mental illness are not all crazy. Psychology studies the working of the mind. All minds. Even your inadequate offering, Devon Dare. As I stated before, psychopathy and sociopathy will be touched upon. Matters of religion will be reserved for teachers better suited to their instruction."

Casey hid a chuckle behind her hand. *Devon's so confused, he looks like a dog when he forgot where he buried his bone.* Devon glared at her as he took his seat.

Dr. Bridges tapped his white board to gather attention and introduced facts about depression.

Casey jotted notes. Fatigue. Sleep issues (too much or too little). Loss of interest in pleasurable activities. Muscle aches. Irritability. *I could probably tell him a few things he might not know.*

"Depression is a disease that can be treated. With proper therapy and medication, prognosis is good," he said.

Or psychiatrists throw medicine at someone without realizing the consequences. Her mother's naked body remained a bitter image stuck in her brain. *No wonder we have no friends to the house. Never know what you'll find at the crazy Adams home.*

The room's warmth wrapped about her like a security blanket. Her thoughts slowed, and Dr. Bridges' words devolved into a monotonous drone.

She revisited the picnic, but her mother sunbathed beside her, nude. "Mom, what the heck." White petals fell from the tree and blanketed them with fragrance. The petals turned cold, and they shivered beneath a layer of snow. "Mom, we have to get home. Where's Dad?" Her mother mouthed secrets. Casey struggled to understand. Her mother's face fell toward her, half-consumed by squirming, waxy maggots.

Casey jolted awake with a scream. Everyone stared gape mouthed or chuckled. Her shame burned, and she hunched into a ball.

I wish the invisibility that used to cloak me wrapped me now. The indentations on Jaimie's face indicated an interrupted rest. She mouthed, "Are you okay?"

Casey shrugged. Dr. Bridges referred to papers at his podium. "Ms. Adams, is it? Are you well, or do you need a break?"

As though squeezed in a vice, Casey's throat constricted and prevented a response. She slunk further into her seat. *Don't cry in class.*

Jaimie scraped her chair as she stood. "She's fine. Darned spider. I got it though. Do you teach about arachnophobia because I think we have a prime candidate for a case study."

Uneasy laughter. The professor tapped his foot until the room quieted. "In the next section, we cover phobias. I expect you will do as your excellent friend suggests, Ms. Adams, and volunteer for a case study."

The laughter renewed, louder. Dr. Bridges raised his hands. "Calm down, now. Please ignore any future arachnids and let's return to our lesson."

After class, Casey asked Jaimie to wait outside. As he walked by the Emo girl, Devon whispered. "Maybe Little Miss Casey's a psychopomp?"

The Emo girl sneered at Devon. "Didn't you hear the self-important professor? Is the word you're looking for psychopath?"

Devon snorted, his gaze lingered. "Whatever."

Sheepish, Casey loitered near the whiteboard as Dr. Bridges gathered his materials. "I'm so sorry, Professor, for disrupting class."

He studied her with a steady gaze. "Is there something troubling you, Ms. Adams? I do have office hours posted if so."

"No, I just wanted to apologize." Her throat closed again, and she turned to leave.

"You know, Ms. Adams, I am happy to refer you to one of my colleagues if you require professional services."

She spun, mouth slack. *Me? My mom's the crazy one.* She gulped. "You know, I do have a question for you, sir. How long does postpartum depression last if properly treated?"

With a half-smile, he nodded. "Each case is individual, of course, but it is my understanding with treatment, postpartum depression usually resolves after three months. I imagine you have a reason for the question?"

He stole a glance at her flat stomach.

She backed away.

"Just curious. What if it lasts longer?"

He shrugged. "A different diagnosis would most likely be in order."

She edged toward the door.

"Maybe I'll visit you during your open hours. I don't want to take up your time."

His brows met, but his eyes sparkled. "This is someone important to you. Would you like to go somewhere to talk now? I have a bit of time before my next lecture."

What? Did I hear him correctly? "No, I'll make an appointment for office hours." She turned to leave.

Dr. Krochalis blocked the exit, arms crossed over her stomach. "Hello, Geof. Ms. Adams. We are going to the Thai place. Care to join in the culinary fun?"

Casey stepped aside. *Don't want to interfere with their conversation.*

"Unfortunately, Jeanne, Ms. Adams was just trying to make a gracious exit. Apparently, it isn't only spiders that frighten her." He chuckled.

Casey's mouth fell open again at his banter. *Wait. Do they want me to go with them?*

Dr. Krochalis shrugged. "Our loss. I'd enjoy getting to know you better, young lady."

Casey raised her eyebrows into her bangs. "Me? You want to get to know me?"

Both professors wore amused expressions. He said, "Of course. You're one of our best students. Loads of potential.

"We've all noticed. At a school this size, the cream of the class becomes apparent early on."

Casey ducked and a cascade of blonde obscured her discomfort. Her voice sounded thin and childish. "Well, thank you. Perhaps another time, but my friend Jaimie's waiting for me now."

Dr. Bridges nodded. "We'll hold you to that, won't we Jeanne?"

"Indeed."

"Well, thanks." Casey's head bowed as she left the classroom. The internal bees quieted as Casey tried to work out the exchange with her favorite professors. She wandered outdoors. She followed a familiar path to the bench where she often sat with Jaimie after class.

Jaimie approached, arms crossed, hands engaged in a nervous rhythm. "Hey." Jaimie's voice sounded strained. "Um, Casey, darling, try not to be upset."

Casey's stomach clenched. *When does anyone start a conversation with "don't be upset" unless there's a reason for them to be upset?*

Jaimie slid beside her on the bench. "I'm not sure how to tell you this, but I think you need to see." Jaimie held out her phone toward her.

A photoshopped image of Casey's head stared from the screen.

Spiders circled, bearing lecherous cartoon smiles. The Casey in the screen wore a sexy "Miss Muffet" costume, exposing another person's buxom, long-legged body. The image bore the caption, "Let's frighten Ms. Casey away."

Casey snorted. "Where'd you get that?"

Jaimie's twitch returned. "It's on the school social media home page."

Casey's phone vibrated. A message from Tim read, "Are you okay? I saw a weird Instagram."

Casey's mouth dropped. "Is it on Instagram, too?"

Jaimie nodded. She avoided eye contact. Her voice hushed. "And Twitter. Hashtag Casey does spiders."

Casey shook her head, mouth agape. Betrayal beat in her rapid heartbeat. *Someone from psychology class hates me. But why? I never hurt anyone.* "Who'd do this? And why?"

Jaimie stared, wide-eyed. "I'm sorry, honey. I don't know."

Students walked by. Some stole glances at Casey. Others pointed and snickered. Unaccustomed to notoriety or simple attention, Casey shrunk into the wooden slats, into her coat and behind her books and folders. She longed for a return to anonymity.

Jaimie slapped the bench. "I bet it's that Annamarie."

Casey raised her eyebrows. "Why on earth would Annamarie do something like this?"

The number of views of the Miss Casey meme grew to over 100. "I barely know her."

"Bet she's jealous. I mean, she's got her manicured nails all over Devon, and all he does is stare at you."

Casey's perspective swirled. "What are you talking about? Jaimie, that's crazy. I don't know Annamarie outside of class, and Devon's never even talked to me."

"It's true, though."

Devon Dare, interested in me? That's ridiculous.

A group of upperclassmen leered. "Looking good Miss Casey!"

Tim saw this. Sweat prickled her scalp. The world swirled. *How can this be happening?* Campus colors blended into one dark pinpoint. Their words echoed and settled into a sad weight in her stomach. Casey leapt from the bench and ran to the restroom.

Jaimie yelled, "Are you okay?"

"No, I'm going to be sick."

And she was.

Chapter Fifteen

Sharing Dreams

The girls met with Tim and Red for lunch at the Willows. Jaimie's face pinched with concern. "Hey guys. Where's Ryan?"

Red shrugged. "Haven't seen him since Saturday. Have you?"

Jaimie shook her head, studied the menu, and blinked back tears. "Nope. He's not answering my calls or texts." She bounced her foot with agitation. "You think he's okay, right?"

Tim nodded. "I'm sure he is, but it's weird not hearing from him."

Yawns circled the table. Red and Jaimie tapped the tabletop like competing bongo players. Dark circles ringed their eyes.

Tim gazed, glassy-eyed at Casey. "You doing okay, Case?"

Casey's sidelong smile hid concern. "I guess I'm okay. Why'd you ask?"

He reached and ran a finger along her cheek. "Beautiful girl, you look sadder than usual."

Casey recoiled from his unaccustomed touch. "I'm fine."

At least he's not bringing up the embarrassing online thing.

Red's nostrils flared. "How about you, Tim-Tim? How are you doing?"

"Actually, I'm worried about Tommy." He stared at Casey as he spoke. "He's acting weird. Won't leave his room. Lost, sort of. Doesn't want to eat. He's downloading Native American drum songs and screeching in his room. Gone all native, stomping about."

He caught a lock of Casey's hair and ran his fingers through it. "You sure you're okay, Casey?"

Casey studied the rhythmic pattern of Jaimie foot. "Just a headache I guess."

Tim reached into his pocket. "I've got some ibuprofen. It might help with the headache." He slid the bottle across the table to her.

Casey ignored Tim's advance. Her head pounded. The sense of unease she had pushed from her thoughts demanded attention.

Tim continued. "My folks are worried to death about Tommy. Blaming me—well, blaming us. Stages of Grief. They're saying they never should have allowed Tommy to be a part of the band."

Red scoffed. "What's being in the band got to do with anything?"

"Don't know, but I don't even recognize my kid brother. Not since—"

He cleared his throat. He blinked rapidly, and his voice sounded husky. "Saturday." He shifted closer to Casey.

He whispered, "Not since we went to that stupid circle thing."

Everyone fidgeted in their seats.

Red whispered, "I've not heard from Rom since then, either. He's usually such a clingy pain in the butt, so it's strange not to have twelve texts a day." She wiggled her fingers. Dust danced in the golden light. "I called him. He went on about the moon, said he knew what he was." Red closed her eyes, but her fingers strummed an invisible harp.

Jaimie rested her head on folded hands. "Well, what is he?"

Red snorted. "Crazy? I don't know."

"Didn't he say? You could ask."

"Jaimie, Rom's always been a bit off. I'm not sure I want to know what he thinks he is."

The group fell silent while the waitress brought drinks and walked away. Jaimie grabbed her cell phone. "I'm calling Ryan." She giggled, eyes wide. "You guys have me a tad concerned."

"I bet he won't answer." Tim said between yawns.

She dialed and sighed. "Hi! It's Jaimie. Call me, please. We're worried about you."

She thumped the fork with her thumb.

Casey tapped her chin. Her heart raced, but she kept her voice steady. "You know what I think? I'm guessing none of us have slept much. We're all over-reacting and need a good night to reset."

Red's musical laugh filled the room. "As if! Any time I close my eyes, I see that witch in my dreams."

Jaimie and Tim sat poker straight.

Cold dread crept up Casey's spine. "Witch?"

"Long red hair, eyes green light bright. Fricken flying from cloud to cloud, disappearing and reappearing."

Chills covered Casey, and her hair stood on end. In her few moments of sleep, a woman with long, dark hair haunted outside her window. She moaned and wept, bony finger pointed at her.

When the woman walked away, she disappeared between street lights and reappeared in another spot.

Jaimie's uncontrolled twitch returned. "A witch is in my dream, too, but I'm underwater and her hair is long and white as a Beluga whale's underbelly."

As a corpse's stare.

Tim sounded entranced.

"It's blonde like Casey's, and she laughs in the ruin of a Grecian temple. She steps behind one column and appears from another. Long gown sweeping the ground."

Red wiggled her fingers. "Her nails are sharp as talons."

Jaimie added, "Polished like gems."

Red as blood.

Tim sighed and closed his eyes. "She's beautiful."

She's a disaster.

They all shuddered, gooseflesh visible.

A loud buzz and pressure assailed Casey's head. She asked, "What's it mean? Sounds like she's in all of our dreams. Same woman, different appearance. Different places." She chewed her lip.

"I wonder if Tommy, Rom, and Ryan met her, too."

Chapter Sixteen

Artistically Speaking

Two men argued in the dorm hallway outside Ryan's room. One wore a NorEast hoodie and leaned against the wall, hands in his pockets. "Dude, calm down," he said. "You two have been roommates for two years now, right? Is this really different?"

The red-faced man yelled, "Yes, that's what I'm telling you. He's gone insane. Won't sleep. Plays music all night, and I'm getting high from all the paint fumes."

Tim rested a hand on Casey's shoulder. He whispered, "That's Ryan's roommate."

Jaimie looked at Tim, then squinted at the unhappy men. "The other guy's a Resident Assistant, right?"

Tim nodded. "I think so."

The R.A. said, "Look, I'll do what I can, but the dorms are filled. See if you can work something out together."

Red-face shook his head and motioned with his hands. "Man, this sucks." He skulked away.

The R.A. ran a hand through his hair. He swept a tired glance at them and sighed.

"No women in the dorms, Tim. You know that, right?"

"Yeah. We're here to check on Ryan. Worried about him." He pointed to the door.

The R.A. blew a puff of air and shrugged. "Maybe it will help. Guess you heard his roomie. Guy's pretty ticked." He addressed the girls. "Be out of here before dinner." They nodded.

The group exchanged worried glances and walked to Ryan's room. Tim knocked.

No answer.

He tried the handle. It turned, unlocked. "Ryan, It's Tim and the girls."

The joyful tones of Vivaldi's "Spring" greeted, while turpentine and oil paint made her nose burn. Their eyes watered from the fumes. Jaimie rushed ahead. Red and Casey lingered behind Tim.

Painted canvases lined the walls and rested atop the desk beneath Ryan's loft bed. An abstract in greens and blues with a shock of gold made Casey think of a Hans Christian Andersen story she loved as a child. Beside it, a wolf bayed at a full moon.

In the next, a castle served as a backdrop for a knight atop a stallion. A maiden cried on a lonely hill nearby. In another, muted gardens hid fairies, and in another, Native Americans danced around a vibrant red bonfire.

Casey knelt for a better look at a haunting image. Ghostly people followed a woman to a graveyard. She buried her face in pale hands. Blonde hair spilled to obscure details.

Her bare feet kicked dust clouds which glistened in the moonlight. She wore a white, old-fashioned nightgown. Casey touched the canvas. *I have a nightgown like that. It's my favorite.* She pressed her fingers to trembling lips, contemplating the darkest patch on the canvas, the gothic-inspired cemetery.

How does she know where she's going if her eyes are covered like that?

Red knelt beside her and gazed with a lost expression at a ring of stones atop a grassy knoll. Sheep dotted the foreground. Lightning illuminated a twilight sky. Casey noticed a tear trickle over Red's pronounced cheekbone.

Jaimie prattled to Ryan. "We've been worried about you, Ryan. Nobody's heard from you. You don't answer your calls or texts."

Ryan nodded, gaze intent on the canvas he painted. Another bonfire crackled to life in the center. From the wooden base, eyes stared above toothy grins.

Casey shivered and turned from their scrutiny.

Tim leaned on the wall. "Ryan, when's the last time you ate?"

Ryan paused, grunted, and returned to painting.

Jaimie asked, "Do you want me to bring something for you to eat?"

Ryan glanced at her and blinked as though he'd only just registered her presence. "Hey, Jaimie. Could you get me some new oils? I need more red. A lot of red."

Jaimie's brow crinkled as she frowned. "What about food? Are you hungry?"

Ryan blinked eyes sticky from lack of sleep yet glowed with a zealous light. "Just the paint, please. Thanks, doll." He returned to his painting.

Tim stepped close and rested a hand on Ryan's shoulder.

Ryan startled.

With quiet words, Tim said, "You need sleep, food, and a shower. Can't your painting wait until you take care of yourself?"

"No. I've been given inspiration. I'd be a fool to ignore it."

Red cleared her throat. "Ryan, have you dreamed about a witch?"

Ryan grimaced. "A what? A witch? I have no idea what you're talking about."

Jaimie pointed to Ryan's canvases. "Who's inspiring you?"

Ryan held his brush before him, a weapon and a shield. "Get out. I need to concentrate."

Jaimie's eyes widened and her lip quivered.

Ryan allowed his brush to fall to his side. "I'm sorry, but I need to work. Kindly leave."

His fevered approach herded the women toward the door.

Tim interposed. His husky form stymied the artist. He put his palms toward Ryan to calm him.

"We'll leave, but Jaimie's right. We're worried about you. Please eat something and get some sleep."

"Yeah, sure." He waved paint-splattered hands above his unbrushed hair. "Jaimie, red paint, 'kay? They sell it at the student union. Thanks." He slammed the door behind them.

Jaimie stared, mouth wide and dumbfounded. Her abundant nervous energy transformed into staggered, choppy breaths. Her mouth hung open.

Casey rested a hand on her friend's shoulder. Jaimie leaned her head on Casey's shoulder and snuffled tears.

Tim shook his head and huffed.

With a giggle, Red said, "Gee, that went well."

Chapter Seventeen

Rom's Room

Tim put an arm around Jaimie and Casey and guided the girls to the elevator. His finger hovered over the buttons. His jaw clenched. "Let's check on Rom."

They exited on the third floor and hurried to Rom's room. Rom answered before they knocked. An uncharacteristic grin split his face.

"I thought I heard you," Rom said.

Red tipped her head to look up at him. "Heard us? We didn't say anything. Heck, we didn't even knock."

Rom's smile broadened to reveal all his teeth. "Red, why you look good enough to eat." He bent and sniffed her head.

She stepped behind Tim.

"Rom," Jaimie said, "can we talk with you a minute?"

"Bout what, sugar lips?"

Jaimie blinked and frowned.

Tim scowled. "Rom, what's gotten into you?"

Rom's expression soured. He tucked his unshaven chin, eyes narrowed, stance aggressive.

"What's gotten into me?"

His barked laugh startled Casey. She shivered. *Rom's always been a bit odd, but now he's creeping me out.*

With a sweep of his hand and a bow, Rom invited them into his room. The third floor boasted private rooms, small, but roommate-free. Casey wrinkled her nose, assaulted by a corn chip type smell. Heavy curtains lent the vibe of a wild thing's den. The room needed to be cleaned and organized. Books teetered in stacks in the corners and closed in the already small space. The trash bin overflowed with takeout boxes and chewed chicken bones.

Under the loft bed, a sleeping bag lay rumpled. Pieces of Rom's drum kit spread across the loft bed and at the foot of the ladder.

The computer revealed a website concerned with astronomy before it converted to the Stages of Grief screen saver. Papers scattered across the desk displayed Rom's bold handwriting.

"You asked what's gotten into me," Rom paced before them. "I'll tell you, I think it's invigoration. It's like my blood is the ocean, and it feels the seasons. It cries out." He pointed his chin toward the ceiling and howled.

Red took the only seat and stared as though she observed an animal at the zoo. Nervous twitches seized Jaimie, but Tim stood like a sentry before Casey.

Rom laughed. "Do you get it, girls?"

Tim's voice reverberated with authority. "Are you high, Rom?"

The unnerving smile returned to Rom's face. "Nah, I'm not high. Just seeing things as they are for the first time."

Red leaned forward, elbows on her knees. "And how are they, Rom?"

He stalked to her seat and knelt before her. He closed his eyes, nostrils flaring. "Do you know, I loved you?"

Red stiffened but did not respond.

"Yep, I did, but you didn't give me the time of day." He touched her cheek.

She recoiled.

His smile returned. "Don't worry, little Red. I know why now. You and I are different kinds entirely. You just recognized it before I did. Clever of you, really. How'd you know, or is it that famous woman's intuition at work?"

Tim tensed as though prepared to fight.

"No matter," Rom said and returned to his feet with a fluid movement. "It is what it is. I think I've found another like me, though."

Jaimie sounded young and confused.

"Oh? Rom, do you have a girlfriend?"

Rom clasped his hands behind his back.

"I guess you could call her that."

Red cleared her throat. "Do I know her?"

The smile that split his face returned, and Rom laughed. "Jealous? You should be." He yawned and stretched his lips back with exaggeration. "You know her. You all do. She told me."

Casey shivered with foreboding. "Who is she?"

"We'll all know her name when she's ready. She's mysterious, the moon sliding behind the sun's shadow. It will be time for her to shine soon."

Jaimie sidled toward Tim.

Red stood, stretched onto tiptoes, all lean dancer's body. "We just wanted to make sure you were okay. We were worried. Hadn't heard from you and all. Now we know why. You're caught up in your dreams, right? In love with the witch who disappears into the standing stones."

Rom pulled his lips into a sneer. "Jealousy does not suit you, Red."

"Neither does your new brutishness, Rom." She turned to the door.

Rom said, "She's not a witch, you know. She's a goddess."

Jaimie gasped.

"Wait. Are you in love with the woman from our dreams?"

Tim narrowed his eyes.

Casey trembled, an inexpressible dread seized her midsection.

In love with her? I think she'll devour us all if she can.

Rom chuckled, all brilliant teeth and fever-bright eyes. "Aren't you?"

Chapter Eighteen

White Buffalo Woman

Anemic autumn sunlight shone bright but without warmth. They blinked and shielded their eyes.

"We look like we've just crawled out of a cave," Red ran a hand through her hair.

She's right. They were all pale from lack of sleep, blurry eyed, and unsteady on their feet.

Jaimie covered a yawn. "Coffee?"

Red shrugged. "Sure." Leaves crunched as they dragged their feet to the Brew Two.

Cheerful and caffeinated baristas smiled as they crafted coffee confections. Casey sipped her caramel latte and ignored the pang of guilt that gnawed since she plunked down the payment. *I work hard. A splurge once in a while isn't going to kill anyone.* They sipped. Folk music played through the speakers.

Jaimie jiggled as she sipped her double shot espresso.

Tim removed the plastic lid and studied his coffee cup with a frown. He cleared his throat. "I'll be honest, ladies, our visits this afternoon have left me more worried than before."

Jaimie's eyes threatened a wave of tears. Red sighed.

Casey fought nausea. She checked her cellular for messages. *Nothing. Guess everyone's okay at home.* She smoothed her paper napkin and set it at a right angle with the phone.

"I've known Ryan for two years now. Good guy. I've never seen him act like he did today." He rubbed the stubble on his chin. "Don't know Rom as much, but none of their behavior seems normal. Not Ryan's or Rom's. Not my kid brother's either."

Red nodded. "Rom's always been odd, but he seemed really off today. Made me a bit uncomfortable. Unnerved, you know?"

Jaimie sent her hair over her shoulders. "Rom made me uncomfortable, too, like he was too intense or something."

Red asked, "And what was that nonsense about loving the woman from our dreams? It does sound like he met the same witch, doesn't it?"

Tim stood and brushed cookie crumbs from his pants. "I'm going home to check on Tommy. Bet he's met the hag, too, and she's messing with him."

Casey blurted, "Want company?"

He paused, then said, "Sure, if you want to come. I'd love—"

He cleared his throat. "—if you'd come along."

Casey blushed as his gaze lingered.

"Can I come, too?" Jaimie asked.

Red's gaze shifted as she stood. "Me, too? I want to see how the little dude's doing and ask if that witch is in his dreams like she's in ours." She rubbed her temple. Her voice quieted, "Besides, I don't really want to be alone right now."

Casey jolted. *I feel the same way. Just not used to Red being anything but tough.*

Tim consulted his watch. "Tommy should be home from school soon. I could drive."

"My brother and sister should be home soon, too, so I'd better follow you. I'll leave from your place. I don't think your folks live far from my home."

"Wouldn't it have been something if we'd have met sooner?"

You wouldn't have noticed me then. Nobody did, except my family. She placed a hand on his arm, grateful for his solid warmth. "Well, I'm glad we met now."

Color rose in his cheeks, and he studied the clouds.

Red cleared her throat. "Well, not to break up this mutual admiration festival, but the daylight is growing pale, and I'm getting old."

Jaimie giggled. "I'll drive with Casey if you can give me a ride back to campus after, Tim?"

Tim shrugged. "Sure."

While Casey followed Tim's van to his parents' house, Jaimie prattled. "I think Tim's got a major crush."

"So you've been saying."

"Don't you see the puppy eyes he's giving?" She fidgeted and adjusted in the seat as if uncomfortable.

Casey pressed her lips tight. "You're crazy, Jaimie."

She laughed. "So I've heard."

They drove to a blue-sided two story with white shutters and a well-tended lawn. "Welcome." Tim smiled. He led the way to the front door. "Mom, I'm here. I brought some friends."

His mother embraced her son and stood on tip-toes to kiss his cheeks. "How did you grow so much already? You only live down the road, but you look a foot taller."

He grinned. "Maybe you're shrinking, Mom. Ever think of that?"

"Oh, you!" She patted his elbow. "Hello Red! Nice to see you again."

Her smile grew pinch-lipped.

Wonder if Tim's mom's being honest. She doesn't look too pleased to see Red.

His mother turned a more genuine smile on Jaimie and Casey. "But who are these lovely ladies?"

Tim introduced Jaimie. He grabbed Casey's hand as he said, "And this is Casey."

Her eyebrows arched above widened eyes. "Oh? Is this the famous Casey I've heard so much about? Tim and Tommy tell me your family lives close by. Did you go to High School with Tim?"

Heat rose in Casey's face. She pulled her hand from Tim's. "I was an underclassman. Tim's two years older than me."

"Did you know Tommy then?"

Casey shook her head. "Only from meeting the band."

Tim cleared his throat. "Speaking of Tommy, is he home from school?"

His mother narrowed her eyes. "He's in his room. He missed school again today. Said he was sick. He's abed listening to tribal music."

She leveled a weighted glare at her son. "Again."

"Mind if we go up and check on him?"

"I guess that's okay. Don't tire him out though."

She wiped her palms on her thighs. "I'll have cookies ready by the time you're back. Chocolate chip okay?"

"They're great, Mom." He kissed her head.

They followed the uneven tones of Native American chants to a wooden door marked "Tom." Tim knocked. "Tommy?"

Tommy's voice sounded whiney. "I'm still not feeling well, Mom. Not hungry. Sorry. I just want to rest."

"Tombo, Come on. It's me, your big bro. Do you really think I sound like Mom? Never mind. Don't answer that. The girls and I were thinking of you and stopped by. Can we come in?"

Shuffles. "Just a minute." Tommy opened the door, blinking in the brighter light. His appearance surprised Casey.

She covered her mouth, then dropped her hand. *Don't want to embarrass him.*

Unshowered, wan, pale, and glassy-eyed, Tommy epitomized strung out. His room stank of burnt sage, a pungent reminder of the bonfire ceremony.

Tommy turned the music lower and sat cross-legged on his bed. "What's up? Why are you here?"

Tim sat on the bed too. "Mom said you missed school. Why's that?"

"Just not feeling it, you know?"

"No, dude, I don't know. She's worried about you, said you've been acting strange."

Tommy stretched his arms.

"She doesn't understand. I've finally come alive, like I was asleep and now I can see the world and my place in it. Can't you? I mean, all of you have to feel it, too, right? Like there is a pulse in everything, and we run through the veins of creation, Mother Nature's lifeblood."

"That's mighty profound, little brother."

"It means lots more than anything they can teach me in school."

"School's important, too. How else are you going to get a decent job?"

Tommy grew louder. "I've got music."

Red ran a finger through a tray of beads and left a snake-like track. "What are these for?"

Tommy jumped from the bed and grabbed her hand. "I'm learning how to do native beadwork." He pulled her to his closet and opened the door. "See?"

He pulled out boxes filled with beaded collars and small leather pouches on beaded cords.

"You made these?"

"Yeah. Working on them. Something I feel I have to do, you know? Do you like them?"

She held a green and yellow bracelet up to a slit of light from Tommy's drawn blinds. "Sure do."

She ran her fingers over the leaf pattern. "When did you learn how to do these?"

Tommy scratched his elbow. "I couldn't sleep Saturday night. It was too late to play. Mom would have killed me if I made that much noise. She had these beads in her craft closet, and I searched native crafts online."

Red's mouth dropped open. "You made all of these since Saturday?"

Tommy nodded.

Red scrutinized the handiwork. "Wow! I can't believe you're this good at beading when you just taught yourself. Jaimie, Casey, look at these."

The bumps of a beaded white owl medallion rose beneath Casey's fingertips. Amber for the beak and talons and red for the eyes gave the piece character. *Feels like the tiny dried corn we hang on the door to decorate for autumn.*

Tim tapped his foot. "They're very nice, Tommy, but you still need to go to school. Get your degree. College. The whole kit-n-caboodle, bro."

"I hear you, Tim. I've got this figured out, though. I'm telling you." Tommy rested his hands on the girl's shoulders. "Ladies, keep those. They're for you."

He smiled at Casey. "That one's yours." He nodded to the black leather with white owl beads.

He removed a silver and black beaded bracelet with a pewter dagger medallion dangling from its center and handed it to his brother. "For you, Tim."

Tim closed his eyes and sighed. "It's really nice, Tommy, but..."

"No buts. I heard you about school. I also heard what our inner spirit voices have to say. That's why I made these." Tommy smiled.

Jaimie used her teeth to tie her bracelet on her wrist. The blue and green beads looked like raindrops. "I have a question for you. Have you been having weird dreams?"

Casey stiffened and anticipated Tommy's response.

"I don't know. I guess so." He scratched his head. "Well, maybe not weird but really intense. Why?"

Tim said, "We've noticed our dreams are a bit weirder since Saturday."

Tommy shrugged. "I've always had strange dreams."

"Anything different, about them lately, though?"

"Well, they're all about bonfires and the earth. You know, getting to the bones of our existence."

Red struggled with her bracelet. "Any people in these dreams?"

Tommy scratched his stomach. "I don't know." His throat worked as though to keep a secret. "I mean, Sure. I guess so." He cleared his throat and bobbed his head.

"Yeah, there's someone I keep seeing. Sorta."

He lowered his gaze and scratched his belly again. "Not that I want to or anything. It's not like I control my dreams or anything, you know." He chewed his lip. "Why?"

Tim said, "We all have a common visitor, and we wondered if you do, too."

Tommy tied the bracelet on for Red. "Who's that?"

"I don't know her name."

"Her? The woman? Yeah, I've been dreaming about a lady. I think she's the White Buffalo Woman. I've been looking her up online."

Jaimie tapped her foot, anxious. "So she is in your dream? What's she like for you?"

His eyes took on a far-away look. "Beautiful and wise. She sings to animals and can disappear when she wants. Then reappear in a different place. It's pretty cool, y'know."

Jaimie trembled. "Do you get the impression she might not have the best of intentions? Like, she's trying to use you for her own purposes?"

Tommy grinned as he spread his arms wide. "She can use me any way she wants. If I'm clay, I'm hers to mold."

He snatched a piece of rawhide and hummed as he lined up beads for his next bracelet. "I've got stuff to do, so if you don't mind."

He pointed to the door.

Tim closed his door behind them. They wore worry upon their brows as they left.

Chapter Nineteen

School Is Important

Fresh-baked cookies cooled on racks on the dining table. Tim's mom wiped her hands on a flowered apron right out of a 1950's sitcom.

Casey stepped forward, hands twisted into trembling knots. Her voice shook as she said, "Thank you for your hospitality."

"You're welcome any time, my dear, but you're staying for cookies, right?"

Casey stared at the flooring. Hardwood with a nice waxy shine. "No, I'm sorry, I need to get home." She pushed aside the sense of urgency in her gut.

"Wait, please," Tim's mom wrapped a laden paper plate with a napkin. "Take these with you. I insist."

Casey stammered, "Well, thank you. That's very kind." She accepted the warm pile.

She felt the weight of the woman's attention. "My little brother and sister will sure appreciate them."

"How old are they?"

Casey told her and thanked her again. "I have to get home and check on them."

"I hope they'll like the cookies. Be safe. It was nice to meet you."

Tim walked with her and opened her car door. "Thanks for coming to check on Tommy." He leaned on the open door and cleared his throat. "Casey, what's your take on what's going on?"

She shook her head. "I don't know." *I don't like it though.* "You're right, you know. Tommy needs to finish school. Do you think he'll really drop out?"

He shrugged, chest filled with a deep sigh. He rubbed his eyes. "I can't make him go to school. Gosh, I wish I wouldn't have allowed him to attend that bonfire. I didn't know." Worry filled his eyes.

"Me, either. Tim, I don't know what's going on, but it's not your fault, what's happening with Tommy."

"Thanks, Casey." He stammered, "Do you think it's a coincidence, all of these changes in us?"

Casey bit her lip and shook her head. "No, I don't. I think we both know there is something going on. We can all feel it. I don't know what it is though." She glanced at her phone. *Getting late.* "See you Wednesday, okay?"

He straightened but didn't close the door.

"Casey, I know everything is complicated right now, but I can't keep waiting for a perfect moment since there don't seem to be many of them, y'know?

"So I wondered, can I take you to dinner sometime? Maybe a movie?"

Cold air rushed Casey, and she stiffened. *I can't believe it. Jaimie was right. Or was she?* Her voice quivered. "Like, a date? Are you asking me on a date?"

Tim's cheeks colored, and he chuckled. "Yes, a date. Will you go out with me?"

Will it be awkward? Will he try to hold my hand or kiss me? Stop it. You like him. Deep breath. "Sure, I'd like that." *My first date.*

Tim's eyes brightened. "Great! Um, is tomorrow okay? I could pick you up after you're done at work?"

Casey blushed deeper at his eagerness. *I know Jaimie's been telling me this is going to happen, but now that he's asked, I'm trembling.* Through a grin, she repeated, "I'd like that."

"Great. I'll call you tonight. Think about where you'd like to go."

She nodded, unable to make eye contact. She placed her hands in their familiar spots on the steering wheel and squeezed. A euphoric laugh threatened to burst.

How can I be happy when so much is strange in our lives?

He closed the door and patted the door frame as though reluctant to allow her to leave.

Goofy grin in place, he raised his hand. "Thanks! You gave me something to smile about, Casey."

You gave me a smile, too. She spent the drive home lost in anxious thoughts. *What if this is a mistake? What if the date doesn't work out? Will we still be friends? What if he doesn't want to go on another date? What if I don't want to? Is this a terrible error? Is it too late to cancel? How can I cancel without hurting his feelings? But I think I'd like to go.*

After she parked in her driveway, she dialed Aunt Hettie and left a message. "Aunt Hettie, it's Casey. When you get the chance, please call me. I have a situation that I need your help with. Thanks." *She'll know how to handle this.*

She typed a text to Jaimie. "He asked me on a date. Guess you were right." No response. *She's probably right there with him and can't text back.*

Casey rested her head against the steering wheel and tried to clear her thoughts. When her eyes slid closed, Tim's wide grin greeted her. Balmy butterflies floated in her stomach, welcome and exciting at the sight. She sighed, unable to keep a smile from her face.

Then the family from the ice cream shop loomed. They dripped gore and stared with pale, accusatory eyes. She jolted upright.

Her heart pounded. She cursed and gasped for breath.

She covered her face with her hands and cried.

A knock on her window made her jump. Rachel mouthed, "Sorry," and displayed her palms.

Worry creased deep lines into Rachel's face and her lower lip trembled.

Casey reached for her backpack as a cover to wipe her eyes. She stepped out and hugged Rachel. "You scared me!"

"I'm sorry. I didn't mean to."

She kept her arm around her little sister's shoulders. "I know. I'm a little jumpy is all. What's up?"

Rachel sighed. "Just missed you."

"Oh, wait, I forgot the cookies."

"Cookies?"

Casey returned to the car and handed Rachel the plate. "Chocolate chip. Tim and Tommy's mom made them."

"They smell great!"

Casey giggled. "I know! They made my whole car smell wonderful. I think I'm getting fat just from the scent!"

Before they went inside, Casey turned her sister to face her. "What's going on?"

Rachel chewed her lip. "Malcolm stayed home from school today."

"Why?"

"Mom said she needed him."

He needs school. "I'll talk to Daddy. Don't worry, okay?"

Although a weak smile stretched across Rachel's face, worry lines invaded her smooth brow.

Casey ran a hand down her sister's cheek and kissed her head. "We'll take care of it, really. Hey, I have a secret. Want to know?"

Rachel widened her eyes. "Yes." She breathed deep and leaned closer, a conspirator.

"There's this cute guy at school named Tim. I told you about him and his brother."

"The one you thought I'd like?"

"Yeah, that's Tim's little brother, Tommy."

Rachel held the paper-wrapped plate to her nose. "His mom made the cookies, right?"

"Right. They're in the band I went to see. Well, Tim asked me to go on a date."

Rachel forgot the quiet of conspiracy and yelled, "A date! When? Where are you going? What are you wearing? Oh my gosh, this is exciting!"

Casey laughed as Rachel capered like a spring filly set loose in a paddock for the first time.

She snatched the plate of cookies before they became a casualty to Rachel's enthusiasm. "I don't know the answer to any of those questions yet. Maybe you can help me pick out an outfit?"

Rachel clapped. "Yes, of course I will! Is he really cute?"

Casey nodded and blushed, grateful for the distraction provided by news of her embryonic romance.

The girls froze. Mom leaned in the door frame and scowled.

Casey handed Rachel the plate and whispered, "Take the cookies upstairs and share them with Malcolm, please."

Rachel hurried upstairs, a quiet shadow hidden within shadows.

Hiding is a skill we've all adapted. She flashed a wobbly smile at her mother. *Though I seem to be more visible than I care for these days.* "Hey there, Mom. Glad to see you're feeling better."

Mom narrowed her eyes to piggy slits. "What's that mean?"

Casey's knees wobbled and threatened to pitch her to the floor. "Just, I heard you weren't feeling well. You look like you must be feeling stronger." *Lies. She looks awful.* In a quiet voice, she asked, "Are you?"

Mom's red-rimmed eyes glared. "Where were you?"

Not again. "School, Mom."

She placed fists on amble hips. "Didn't you graduate?"

"I graduated from high school, but now I'm in college."

"Why?"

"Because education is important." She hunched her shoulders to make herself smaller and harder to hit. "Just like you always taught us."

Mom nodded. "Education is important."

Should I? Might as well try.

"Yep, that's what you taught us. It's important that we learn as much as we can. Malcolm, too." Her heart rate increased and sweat trickled down the side of her face. *One wrong word can set her off.*

She swallowed. "He's such a smart boy. You're going to be so proud of him."

Tears dribbled from Mom's eyes. "I have smart kids."

"Yes, you do. That's why we need to not miss any days. Plus, our whole family could get into trouble for truancy if we miss."

Mom rubbed her temples.

"Mom, can I make you some tea? I'll get it before I put on dinner."

Casey winced as Mom placed a hand on her shoulder blade. In a sweet, high-pitched voice, Mom said, "That would be wonderful, my dear. Thank you."

"Sure, Mom." Casey plumped pillows on the couch for Mom before starting the kettle.

If only I could divert every crisis as easily.

As the whistle announced readiness, Casey's phone declared a text from Jaimie. "Figured he would. About time, too! That's cool. We have to talk about Red though."

Another jingle. "And don't have him meet you at your house. LOL."

Chapter Twenty

First Date

Work dragged. Casey filed, dusted, swept, and polished, but the clock remained obstinate in its slow progression. Her mind wandered to preparations. She and Rachel had picked out a breezy pastel skirt and white blouse for the date.

When she called last night, Aunt Hettie had sounded close to tears in her enthusiasm for Casey's outing. "Tell me everything. What's he like? Where's he from? Have you met his family? Are they nice? Casey, this is your first date isn't it? Oh honey!"

Casey laughed. "Take a breath, Aunt Hettie! Sheesh, how am I supposed to keep up if you don't let me answer? He's a sophomore. Yes, I met his family. His younger brother and he are in the band I went to see with Jaimie. Stages of Grief. Remember? He's sweet. Used to play football in high school. No, I don't remember him from high school. Nope, not his brother, either. They're really nice, though."

She had taken a deep breath, but she couldn't keep up with Aunt Hettie's barrage. "Yes, my first date."

Aunt Hettie had gushed, "I can bring you my gold hoop earrings if you want to borrow them."

Casey declined her offer. "Thanks, Aunt Hettie, but I'll wear the pearls Aunt Mae sent when I turned sixteen."

"Those will be perfect."

Casey hoped she didn't detect disappointment in her aunt's voice.

As she shelved books from a wheeled cart at the library, Casey found one with an interesting cover. "Psychopomps and Moirologists" by Katerina Dougherty. She ran her finger along the Victorian inspired artwork.

The mournful scene intrigued her. Organized into geographical regions, the book's chapters read "Portents of Death," "Professional Mourners," "Eulogies, Elegies, and Funerary remembrances," and "Conveyances to the Afterlife."

Almost every section featured "criers," people who saw to the sanctity the deceased's death. In India, women called Rudaali continue to work as professional mourners. Casey rubbed her temples and fought back tears.

What's wrong with me? Weepy again?

Many cultures believed birds and angels conveyed spirits to their next life. No judgements. Just safe passage for the souls entrusted to their care.

Banshees, Wailing Women, and Black Dogs warned of the time of death.

Flowers like Canterbury Bells or Foxglove rang out for the dying. Even the actions of certain beetles foretold of death.

Casey's shift ended, and she rushed home to shower and get ready. As the water rushed over her, she rehearsed conversations. "Thank you for a lovely evening, Tim." *Her heart beat increased. Will he want a kiss at the end of the night? Should I kiss on the first date?*

She loved the way her apple shampoo and conditioner scented her hair. A spritz of perfume and applied makeup instilled confidence. The skirt swished above her knees. *I feel like I could dance in this.* She twirled.

Rachel clapped. "Casey, you look beautiful!"

Malcolm knocked and poked his head around the corner. "Casey, you do look pretty. Are you driving?"

"Yes, I'm supposed to meet Tim at the restaurant at five."

Malcolm twisted his t-shirt over his chin and exposed his belly. "What time is it now?"

"I have to leave in about ten minutes. Why?"

"Um, can you walk there?"

She stiffened. "No, it's too far. What's going on?" She checked for her car.

Not there.

Her heart grew heavy as an anvil in her chest. Her voice trembled. "Where's the car, Malcolm?"

His voice was tiny. "Mom said she needed to go to the store."

His shoulders hunched, and his head hung. "I'm sorry, Casey. I reminded her that you were going out, but she said she had to go."

You've got to be kidding me. "Did she say when she'd be back?"

"No."

Casey dialed her mother's cellular. No answer, as she expected. She left a message. "Mom, when are you coming back? Please call."

Rachel tugged on her sleeve. She pointed to the corner where Malcolm cried, huddled in a corner.

Great. She knelt beside him. "Malcolm, honey, please don't cry."

He sniffed. "I tried to stop her, Casey. Really, I did."

She pulled him into a hug. "You did great. No more tears. We'll figure this out."

For a woman who barely left the couch for the past five years, she sure is agile all of a sudden. Maybe I can ask to borrow Aunt Hettie's car. Shoot, wait. I can't leave the kids by themselves.

The tiredness she had ignored seized her. Her head weighed as heavy as her heart.

She dialed Tim.

"Casey! I can't wait to see you." His enthusiasm brought tears of disappointment. She brushed them away with an angry swipe.

Reluctantly. "Tim, there's a problem."

Silence. *Get it over with.* "I don't have a way to get there."

His breath rushed. "Oh, that's no problem. I'll come pick you up."

She rubbed her temple. "Yeah, see, I can't leave. There's no one to watch my little brother and sister."

Silence. "Oh."

She plucked at her skirt. It drooped instead of swirled. She whispered, "I'm sorry."

"It's all right. Maybe we can try for another time. Take care."

Tears made silent tracks over her flamed cheeks. "You, too." She disconnected. *Why does my life suck so bad?* She rubbed her eyes with the heels of her hands. Mascara marked her wrists, dark as bruises.

Her phone jingled a new text. "Have a great first date, sweetie." Aunt Hettie.

A lump rose in Casey's throat, but she squared her shoulders and wiped beneath her eyes. She turned to her siblings. "What's for dinner? I'm starving."

Rachel frowned. Malcolm grabbed Casey's hand. They made their way to the kitchen.

Very few groceries graced the shelves. "Guess it's PB&J sandwiches again, kids." Casey's stomach rumbled. *I didn't eat all day. Tim had reservations at The Lakefront. I heard their steaks are the best in the state.* She salivated.

"Ugh," Malcolm said, "PB&J again."

Casey's phone vibrated. The caller ID read TIM.

She answered. "Hello?"

"So, you're stuck at your house, right?"

"Yes."

"Well, here's the thing. I really wanted to hang out with you, and I hope you're not just trying to find a way out of going on a date with me. If so, stop me now before I make a real idiot of myself." His nervous chuckle punctuated a pause.

Casey stayed silent.

"Okay, I'm assuming you wouldn't let me be an idiot, right? Anyway, I wondered if I could come there and bring dinner to you and your kid sister and brother? I can pick up a bucket of chicken and biscuits if they like that sort of food. Maybe we can play ball or something."

Geeze, what if Mom pulls the nude model thing again? No way we can meet here. Disappointment tasted bitter. *Still, how do I explain that? 'Gee, Tim, that's cool of you and all, but I have a lunatic mother.'* "I was really looking forward to tonight, actually, Tim, but..."

"Then it's a date. Give me your address."

Shoot. "Well, I'd like for you to visit and all, but..."

His voice deepened, tired. "Casey, you're not just trying to get out of a date with me, are you? If so, please just tell me."

Her stomach lurched. Words flooded from her lips. "No, it's not that at all. I told you, I've been excited about seeing you all day." She straightened her skirt. "Wait, I have an idea. There's a park close by, walking distance. We could meet you there."

"Do you mean Beaver Creek?"

"Yeah."

"Great. See you in about an hour?"

"Perfect."

She smiled. "Do you two want to join me on my first date?"

Chapter Twenty-One

Picnic in the Park

Casey rushed around and gathered items for their picnic. She tossed into a sack a red checkered tablecloth, fruit, mitts, ball, and bat. "Put your shoes on, please," she told the kids.

The mirror revealed smeared makeup. *Well, that's not attractive.* Casey reapplied mascara, concealer, and eyeliner. A smear of frosted lip gloss and spritz of perfume rejuvenated her look. She shrugged. *It'll have to do.* "Rachel, should I change into shorts?"

"No, you look like a princess," Malcolm said, and Rachel agreed.

"Okay, I hope I don't look like I'm trying too hard."

They held hands as they walked to the park and sang a rousing chorus of "The Ants Go Marching." "Sure, hope the ants don't go marching over our lunch," Casey laughed.

"Me, too," the kids giggled.

They kicked the last of autumn's leaves as they passed stands of chrysanthemum and aster. At the park, they covered a picnic table with their cloth and waited.

I hope the kids like Tim.

Birdsong trilled as the sun of an Indian Summer warmed them. Tim arrived dressed in khakis and a loosened shirt, a bucket of fried food in hand. A huge grin threatened to split his face in half as he handed her a bouquet of white carnations wrapped in silvery tissue and bound with a wide bow.

Rachel squealed. "Oh my goodness! Casey, he brought you flowers."

Casey inhaled their spicy fragrance. "I can see that." She smiled at Tim. "They are so pretty and smell great."

He raised his eyebrows. "They take after you then." He laughed as she flustered.

Casey rambled, "I'll put these in a cup of water. They'll be a perfect centerpiece for our dinner. See?"

His eyes twinkled with amusement. "Perfect," but his gaze lingered on Casey, not the flowers. He stepped closer and whispered, "Casey, you look beautiful."

His breath tickled, and she shivered. When he wrapped her in a one-armed hug, she stiffened. *Awkward with the kids around. Still, he sure smells nice, like cedar.* She made introductions as they set the table.

Tim served coleslaw. "I'm really glad to meet you both. Casey's one of my favorite people."

Her cheeks burned. "Want some butter for your biscuits?" Her hair fell in a sheet across her face as Casey slathered the warm buns with butter. *Hope nobody notices my blush.*

Rachel rested her chin on her hand and smiled into Tim's face, her voice higher than usual. "How did you two meet, Tim?" Her lips curled around his name. *I'd say Rachel likes him.*

Malcolm pinched his lips and crossed arms. His eyebrows hung low over narrowed eyes, and he glared as Tim shifted closer to Casey.

Guess Malcolm doesn't share Rachel's enthusiasm.

"Casey came to a 'Stages of Grief' show." He chuckled and brushed a bug from Casey's shoulder. "I thought she was a statue at first. She stood along the side wall away from everyone else. Turns out, she's not fond of crowds and just wanted to be near the emergency exit."

Breathless, Casey gulped. "I never said that."

His eyes sparkled in the dappled sunlight. "You didn't need to." Tim slipped an arm around her shoulders.

Her skin tingled at his touch.

"Your sister is the coolest girl at our school, and that's really saying something special."

He leaned across the table and raised his eyebrows. "There are a lot of kids there, you know, and a lot of them are pretty cool."

Casey's mouth dropped open and her skin burned from the roots of her hair to below her collar bone.

Rachel giggled and twirled her hair. "We like her a whole lot, too."

Malcolm groaned as he climbed from the picnic bench. "I'm going to swing." He stomped his way to the playground.

Casey called, "Are you done eating?"

Malcolm lifted his hand. "Yes. Thanks." He mounted the ladder and slid to the swings.

Tim blinked after him. "I don't think Malcolm likes me all that much."

Rachel waved her hands as though she brushed the idea aside. "Oh, he just takes a little while to get used to new people. He'll love you soon, I bet."

"I'd like that." He studied Casey. "I'd like to be loved."

Woah, cool your jets, mister. You're cute and all, but this is our first date. Casey frowned at her hardened biscuit. *Still, Tim sure is sweet.*

Rachel leapt from the table. "I'll push you, Malcolm."

She winked at Casey before she ran to join their brother at the swing set.

Tim's hand leapt to hold Casey's. *Feels weightier without the kids here somehow.* She shook her head and allowed her hair to snake across her face, pulled her hand free, and rose to tidy up. "Thank you for dinner. It was wonderful."

Tim closed the boxes and stacked them in the bag. "It wasn't what I planned, but I don't mind. Not in the least."

Kids' laughter filled the silent moment.

"Casey, I meant what I told your brother and sister. I like you a whole lot. I just want you to know."

I like you, too, Tim, but I can't tell you that. Not yet.

"How's your brother doing?"

Tim shook the cloth with a chuckle. "He's turning native. He's going on about being a member of the Rainbow Tribe and a part of the vast wisdom of nature. He's really obsessed, but he agreed to finish the school year. Said he makes no guarantees about next year though."

"One day at a time, I guess. As long as he finishes this year, we can work on next."

"Yeah, that's true. We can work on next year when it is closer." He emphasized the word "we."

He held the checkered cloth. "Want to spread this on the grass to sit on?"

Casey shrugged. "Sure. Good idea."

They sat in a shady spot beneath a graceful weeping willow tree. As they stretched out on the cloth, he wiggled his fingers through thick strands of grass.

With each wind gust, leaves swirled through the fragrant air. Her shoulder tingled where his hand had rested.

When the sun slid toward a glorious sunset of amber and gold, Casey sighed. "I guess we'd better get home. Thank you again. We all had a wonderful time."

"Thank you, Casey." He touched a finger to her nose. He stepped back and smiled. "I'm not going to push you, but please let me know if I may take you on another date sometime. Maybe it can be just you and me next time?"

Casey studied his running shoes. "I'd like that."

His tone brightened and his words rushed. "You would? Great! How about Friday? Are you free?"

Gosh, I hope so. She giggled. "I'll let you know. Thanks again for dinner."

He rubbed his neck and shuffled his feet. "Yeah, let me know. No pressure though, like I said."

Casey called, "Rachel, Malcolm, time to go."

He carried the bag of leftovers and she the cup of flowers as they walked to the cars.

He stopped, brow furrowed. "Where's your car?"

Rachel said, "Oh, we walked."

"Walked?"

A cold wash of worry seized her. "Yeah, I told you, we don't live far from here, and I didn't have the car. That's why I couldn't meet you, remember? We'd better get going, though. I'll see you in class tomorrow."

"Don't be silly. I'll drive you home. Hop in."

Shoot. What if Mom's home? Her breathing grew shallow and her heart raced.

Tim grabbed Casey's hand. "Are you okay?"

"I just," *How do I explain this?* "Um, really, we can walk." *When Jaimie came over...* She shuddered. "It's not far."

Tim chewed his lower lip. "I promise, I'm a good driver."

"It's not that. We want to walk."

His brow creased, and he tilted his head like a confused puppy.

"Please." *Don't hate me. Don't ask questions I can't answer.* She trembled. *Please don't think I don't like you because I think I really do.*

Malcolm stepped between them, fists on his hips. He glowered. "She wants to walk."

Tim shook his head and dropped Casey's hand. He whispered, "I'm sorry. I just thought I might help."

Tears threatened. Before they could fall, Casey said, "Thank you, Tim. We have to go now though. We really had a great time."

She felt him watch as they exited. Rachel turned and waved. "Bye! I can't wait to see you again."

Bet he doesn't want to see me again after that weird departure. I probably confused the heck out of him.

She ignored a tear that escaped and dripped from her chin.

His van's engine turned, and gravel crunched beneath tires.

Beep beep. Tim pulled alongside them. "I had a great time, too. Friday, Casey, if you're available, let's go to dinner. I'll make reservations, okay?"

Her mouth fell slack. "Okay."

"And call me when you get home to let me know you're safe, please."

She nodded.

He drove off with a wave.

They waved and continued home.

Rachel interrupted the silence. "Why couldn't he drive us home?"

Casey ruffled her hair.

Cool air brushed across Casey's face. In the driveway, the engine of her car ticked, still warm.

"Mom's home," she struggled to keep the foreboding from her voice.

Chapter Twenty Two

Christmas Come Early

Mom greeted them at the door with a wicked grin. "About time you all got here. I have presents for you."

Packages littered the dining room table, wrapped in thick department store paper bound with glossy ribbons. Mom stood the head of the table. Her hair and makeup shone fresh from a salon appointment. Airbrushed tips glittered on her fingernails.

The kids gasped. Malcolm ran to embrace Mom.

Casey swallowed apprehension. *Reminds me of the Trojan horse.* "What's the occasion?"

Mom cocked her head. "You all are doing so well in school, so these are your rewards."

Rachel clapped. "Can we open them?"

How did she pay for these? Does Daddy know? Casey ran a hand through her hair. "Or do you want to wait for Daddy? He'll be here in about an hour."

"I don't think we have to wait. You can show him your gifts when he gets home."

The kids ripped paper. Shreds flew like confetti at a ticker tape parade.

"Oh, a superhero action figure like the one the toof fairy brought."

"Perfume! Grown up perfume. Smell this, Casey."

"Smells wonderful."

Mom held out a package. "Open yours." Her gentle expression almost eased Casey's anxiety. *Don't think that way or you'll miss when she throws the china at your head.*

Wrapped in purple, the box weighed little. The kids paused as Casey unveiled her gift. She slid her finger along the tape line and received a paper cut. "Ouch." She stuck her finger in her mouth and then dove to replace the paper before the kids saw the contents. Tears obscured her vision, and she blushed from collarbone to hairline. *Surely not.* She peeked again. The contents boasted embarrassing names. She whispered, "Why did you buy this, Mom?"

Her voice dripped like honey from a comb. "You're a grown woman now. We don't need any babies running about, now do we?"

Casey seized the box, ran to her room, and slammed the door. *I've never even kissed a boy. Why would I need a box filled with condoms and sex things?* She dropped the box into the trash can and buried her head under her pillows.

"Why does she hate me?" Casey cried until she drifted to sleep.

Chapter Twenty Three

Family Concerns

The woman waited in her dreams and called to Casey. At her voice, shivers raced along Casey's spine. Tears slid down the woman's pale face and smeared her colors like turpentine dropped on a canvas. "Why do you deny me?"

Rachel called, and the woman in the yard pointed with a finger pale as bone. A wicked smile marred her grief. "No, you leave my sister alone!" Casey screamed herself awake.

"Are you okay, Casey?" Rachel peeked around her bedroom dresser dressed in mismatched fuzzy pajamas and dirty bunny slippers. She appeared younger than her age.

Casey leapt from the bed and scooped Rachel into her arms. *She's all knees, elbows and long limbs, like a filly.* She nestled her nose into Rachel's soft hair. It smelled of the new perfume, citrusy and fresh. Her arms shook. Casey set her sister on the ground. "Gosh, you're getting to be a young lady."

"Are you okay? I heard you crying again."

Casey touched her cheeks and found them slick with tears. "Just a bad dream. Nothing to worry about."

Rachel's eyes grew damp. "You have a lot of them. Bad dreams. I know. I hear you." She pointed. "My bed's right there."

Casey nodded. "Lately, my sleep's been disturbed. I'm hoping it gets better soon."

"Me, too. I don't like seeing you this way."

They sat on Casey's bed in companionable silence until they heard Daddy in the driveway.

Casey asked, "Where's Mom?"

"In the attic. I don't know why."

"Malcolm?"

"I put him to sleep."

Her eyebrows shot up her forehead.

Rachel laughed. "He said his prayer, and I told him a bedtime story. Sang a song and everything, just like you usually do."

Casey patted her sister's back. "Well done. You really are growing up far too fast, you know."

"Nah, just fast enough."

Casey grabbed Rachel's hand and pulled her up. It felt small within her own, a delicate thing to be protected. Their footfalls made little noise as they descended to see their father.

Dad smelled of engine oil as he embraced them. "How are my girls? My charming beauties."

Casey asked, "Want some left-over chicken and biscuits?"

"We had a picnic in the park today with Casey's boyfriend Tim. He's in a band called 'Stages of Grief.' He's really cool." Rachel giggled.

Dad's face grew still. "Rachel, would you mind heating up some chicken for me, please? Thanks love." He took Casey's face in perpetually stained gray hands and whispered, "I thought you had a date tonight? Your first date, right?"

Casey pulled away, a familiar knot in her throat. "It worked out okay. Mom needed my car, I guess, so Tim met us at the park."

When he straightened, Dad stood a full head taller. "Your Mom went somewhere again?"

"Shopping. She brought presents." Casey's face burned as she recalled the gift from her mother.

"I did." Mom's voice sugared and heavy like a Hollywood starlet. She draped against the wall, arm arced over her head. A whiff of Opium perfume burned Casey's nose. Dressed in a black evening gown, Mom sashayed across the floor to her husband. At her throat, diamonds and sapphires sparkled. In a sultry, alto rumble, she said, "Wait until you see what I got for you."

Casey retreated to her bedroom and closed the door. *The witch in the yard is preferable to my mother at the moment.*

On her bed, her forgotten phone displayed a group message.

Red: Need to talk to you all.

Jaimie: What's up?

Tim: You okay?

Red: It's Rom. I'm really getting scared. He just got kicked out of his dorm. Fighting or something. I think he's living in his car.

Jaimie: I haven't seen Ryan in class, either.

Tim: Maybe we should meet. Casey, you with us?

Casey checked the time stamp. Recent. She typed:

Yes, I'm here.

Jaimie: I don't know if I can leave. My parents called. They said they're on their way. Something must be wrong. I wonder if they're bringing my brother, James.

Tim: I can't go into your dorm. They don't let guys in.

Red: What time are your parents coming, Jaimie?

Jaimie: They're on their way. I guess an hour and a half or so.

Tim: It'll take Casey a half an hour to get here.

Casey: What about meeting outside of your dorm at the benches under the pear trees? We'll be able to see when your folks arrive from there, Jaimie.

Jaimie: Great idea.

Red: On my way.

Tim: Me, too.

Casey: I have to check with my parents, but I don't think it will be a problem.

Casey found her parents in the dining room. Mom lit candles in a dusty candelabra as Dad ate reheated chicken from a paper plate. Casey tiptoed to the kitchen where Rachel tidied up the dinner things. Casey whispered, "I'm going to see a couple of friends. You should go to your room and stay inside, okay?"

Rachel clutched her hands like an accomplice. "Oooh, are you going to see Tim?"

Casey raised her eyes to the ceiling. "Yes, and Jaimie and Red, too. I'm leaving a note for Mom and Dad here on the counter, but just so you know, I should be back soon. I have classes early tomorrow."

"Have fun and give Tim a kiss for me."

"Rachel!"

Rachel giggled as she dried her hands. "I'd kiss him if he were my boyfriend. He's cute."

"Oh my goodness, he's not my boyfriend." *She's right, though. He is cute.* Her skin electrified with his remembered touch. *Much nicer to think about Tim than consider the mess we are in.*

As she drove to campus, she recalled his cologne and the way his eyes sparkled when he teased.

As she walked to Jaimie's dorm, leaves eddied tiny dances.

Tim stood and waved. The winds brushed his hair and whipped his jacket tight against his chest. "Casey, over here!" His wide shoulders and straight stance lent an air of protection to their group, like a soldier at attention.

His smile welcomed her, a beacon to the safety of his embrace.

She hurried, a reflection of her quickened heart. He pulled her into his arms for a quick hug.

Casey caught her breath. "What's going on?"

Red scowled and crossed her arms, eyes narrowed. "You read the text messages. You know what's going on."

Jaimie raised her hands as though to ward off danger. "Easy, Red. She just got here."

Tim slipped an arm around Casey's waist "Glad you came. I missed you."

His warm breath tickled her cheek. Casey giggled. "You just saw me, silly."

His gaze did not waver. "Yep, but I missed you the minute I drove away."

Red's scowl deepened. "What's wrong with you two?"

Jaimie chuckled. "Nothing. Nothing is wrong with them." She stepped between Red and Casey. "We're all over-wrought. Any word on Rom?"

She crossed her arms and grimaced. "Like I said, he's been kicked out of his dorm. Nobody's seen him. His car's not in its spot."

Jaimie said, "I stopped by to check on Ryan. The R.A. wouldn't let me in, but he told me Ryan's still acting crazy. His roommate's ticked. Said Ryan still doesn't sleep. Plays music all night long and paints. He doesn't even think he's eating." Jaimie chewed her lip. "I sent food to his room, but all he wants is new paint."

Tim frowned. "Tommy's still acting weird, too, but at least he agreed to finish the school year."

Red kicked a discarded soda can. It clattered into a trash bin. "I'm really tired of this. It needs to stop. I can't keep going this way. Our friends are acting bizarre. I'm not sleeping because of the dreams." Her voice broke, and she cleared her throat.

"I say we find those wackos who ran the ceremony and make them do something to fix this."

Jaimie cocked her head. "What could they do?"

Red's temper flared. "I don't know, but they'd better do something. Things need to go back the way they were. They're why we are in this mess."

They didn't force us participate. Regrettable as our decision may be, we went willingly.

Casey considered the angry furrow between Red's brows. *Don't think she wants to hear that though.* A cool breeze brought a hint of winter. Casey nestled closer to Tim's warmth.

Tim smiled and tightened his embrace.

Red narrowed her eyes and glared at Casey.

What the heck? Red seems angry at me. Why?

Red stomped. "Well, you don't seem all that concerned, so I'm going to my dorm where I'll stay awake most of the night until I fall asleep exhausted to be haunted by that terrible witch with her bloody fingernails. I hate this."

Jaimie called, "Red, please come back."

Red stalked down the path and ignored the call. As she pounded away, she muttered, and angry puffs rose from her mouth and lingered in the chilly air.

Tim squeezed Casey's shoulder. "I'll be right back. Just want to make sure she gets home all right."

Jaimie tapped her chin. "I'm guessing from the arm around your shoulder that your date went well?"

The breeze punctuated the absence of Tim's embrace. "We didn't exactly go on a date."

"What do you mean?"

"Let's just say my mother struck again."

Jaimie's jaw dropped. "Oh no."

"Oh yes. So he met me and my siblings at the park." Casey smiled as she remembered their shared meal.

"Jaimie, he's the sweetest man I've ever met."

Jaimie's smile slid. "Do you think Red feels that way, too?"

Casey's head snapped. "What? Why would she?" She squinted at Red's retreating form. "Doesn't she date Rom?"

"Rom wants to date her, but no. Red and Rom never dated."

Heaviness settled in Casey's stomach. The wind whistled like a tea kettle.

Tempest in a teacup. Casey shivered and her temples throbbed. "If we're done here, I'm going home."

"Casey, I didn't mean to upset you. It's just I've noticed Red flirts with Tim when you're not around." She rested her hands on Casey's shoulders. "I didn't think too much about it before, but she's sure acting bitchy, isn't she?" Jaimie wrapped Casey in a hug. "Listen to me girlfriend. I can tell he likes you. And if it makes you feel better, when Red flirts, he doesn't flirt back."

Casey shivered. *Where's he now? Chasing after Red.* She mustered a wobbly smile. "Thanks. Are you okay if I go?"

"I guess. Why don't you wait though? You can meet my family, and I bet Tim wants to walk you to your car." Her eyes shone with sincerity.

"I'll take a raincheck. Have a good night, and tell Tim I said goodbye, please." Cold bit her nose, the nose Tim pressed when being playful earlier. Her pace quickened.

I just want to get home. Maybe I can sleep without dreaming for a change.

As she hurried, she noticed an older couple who strolled the flagstone walkways. They held hands A young man with sodden, golden-red hair trailed them like a phantom from a Haunted House attraction. His pale, bloated facial features shocked her. His eyes bulged, and his skin distended as though saturated. He opened his mouth, and water flooded over his swollen, purple-blue lips.

Casey ducked her head and ran the rest of the way to the car. Once inside, she locked the door. She could not contain her grief. She wailed and rested her head against the steering wheel, unable to take a proper breath.

She clawed at her throat, suffocated.

His skin, his eyes. Oh, Lord, was it another vision? That poor man! Should I warn him? What on earth would I say?

Her throat burned, and she gulped for air. Her stomach filled with bile, and a wash of tears obscured her vision. She opened the door and vomited on the pavement.

I have to get home. I can't stay here.

Her hands trembled as she turned the ignition key. The engine roared like an anguished cry of an agonized lion. Casey wiped smeared mascara and tears from her face and put the car in gear. She checked the rear-view mirror. A male figure leapt from the sidewalk and headed her way.

Could that be Tim running?

She pulled away without the answer.

Chapter Twenty Four

Missing Persons

Casey rubbed eyes dry and itchy from lack of sleep. She blinked at her reflection in a compact. *They're blood-shot enough for people to suspect I'm high.* Anemic sunlight filtered through trees' emerging skeletons as she waited for Jamie.

Jaimie did not meet her at their usual spot. Casey texted but got no response.

The phone's jingle announced another message from Tim, though. In his earlier texts, he asked why she left without saying goodbye last night. "I ran to see you, but you were pulling out when I got there." *It was him in the parking lot.* "Want to get a soda?"

"I have to get to class. Do you know where Jaimie is though?"

"Maybe her folks are still here. By the way, can I pick you up at five tomorrow?"

Casey stared at the screen. *Are you sure you wouldn't rather pick up Red?* She put the phone into her pocket without answering the text.

With the wooden bench's rugged support, Casey drifted close to sleep. *I should get to class.*

Squirrels chittered on an overhead branch and startled her alert.

Their tails fluffed, clouds of gray, as the two disputed the territory.

"Why can't you both use the branch? Or does it belong to one of you and the other is trying to take over?" she asked.

The squirrels ignored her.

Devon sauntered by with a woman Casey didn't recognize. *Jaimie thought he was interested in me. Ha!*

Devon dropped a newspaper to the ground near her bench. He nodded to Casey. "Pick that up, will you?"

The woman wound her arm around Devon's bicep and frowned. "Is that the spider girl?"

Seriously? Stupid people. 'Frighten Miss Casey away' is still a thing? Like I ever bother anyone.

"Yeah," Devon chuckled and ogled Casey. "She's the spider girl sensation."

His leer made Casey shiver as their laughter echoed. "Doubt she's ever looked as good as she did in that meme, though." He glanced over his shoulder at Casey and winked.

Casey gasped. Blood trickled from Devon's lacerated throat. It pooled in a dark stain that radiated from his collar.

"Devon," she breathed, but he ignored her. She steeled herself and called again. "Devon, be careful, please."

He turned for a moment. Blood gushed from the wound. It pulsed with each depression of his heart. His face paled and his lips turned blue. "Don't worry about me. I'm a big, strong guy." He showed his biceps, winked again, and slipped his hand low enough to cup his date's bottom. She giggled and rested her head on his bloodied shoulder.

Tears came unbidden, and she snatched the paper as a distraction. Casey moved to throw the newsprint in the trash bin.

She froze. "Family of Missing Teen Offers Reward." The article outlined a frantic search for Annamarie Kinley, reported missing from NorEast University on Monday. The family offered ten thousand dollars for any information about her disappearance and prayed for her safe return.

A black and white high school graduation picture smiled from the center of the article.

Casey pulled the image closer. *Is that the Annamarie from Comparative Religions class?* The girl with the lopsided grin in the photo said yes. Cold sweat collected in Casey's hair, and her stomach plunged.

Was she in class Monday? I don't remember.

Annamarie's expression left her uncomfortable.

Wish I could curl up some place safe. A surprising thought seized her.

Her phone weighted her pocket, and she considered the implications of her plan.

So, when I think of safety, he pops to my mind? She texted Tim. "Can we go out after classes end today instead of later?"

His immediate reply, "Of course. Sounds great. Is the Lakefront still okay for dinner? Do you want to go to a movie, too?"

His enthusiastic responses beguiled. *Sorry, Red. Guess he wants to spend time with me.*

She glanced at Annamarie's soulful gaze again *Of course, he might want to spend time with Red, too. Guys can be like that, I think.*

She stifled her insecurity and typed, "Maybe."

A security guard interrupted. "Excuse me, miss. May I please see your student ID?"

She searched her handbag for the lanyard. "Here it is. What's this about?"

"Routine checks." He returned the badge. "You waiting for someone?"

"Yes. I'm meeting my friend." She considered at the clock tower in the center of campus. "Or at least I thought I was. I have to leave for classes in a couple of minutes."

A snowflake danced in the cold northern air with the promise of a new season. Casey shivered.

"Which hall?"

She pointed. "Pausch Lecture Hall."

The guard pocketed his walkie talkie. "I'll walk with you."

Campus activity waned at this time of the day. Few people lingered. "Thanks for the offer, but I can walk on my own."

"I insist."

Casey retrieved her bag and hurried, careful to remain a pace ahead of the officer.

He huffed. "You walk fast."

"Yep." She sprinted up the steps with a half-hearted, "Thanks." She ducked into the lecture hall and sat near the door when her phone jingled.

Jaimie messaged. "Where are you? I need to talk."

Casey glanced at the phone. *Ten minutes until the lecture.* She texted. "Public speaking class. I waited for you, but a security guard got all creepy. What's up?"

"Can you meet me after class? Please."

"Can you wait an hour?"

"Just come as soon as you can."

I hate this class anyway. "Where are you? I'll come now."

"At the hotel with my parents. Room 308."

Wonder what's going on. "On my way."

"Thank you."

Casey gathered her things and hurried to her car. *I have a bad feeling about this.* She drove faster than usual. With trepidation, she knocked on the door of Room 308.

Jaimie answered. Uncombed hair hung in tangles over her shoulders. Her eyes puffed.

"You came." A well burst, and tears flooded her face. She trembled as she hugged Casey.

Holy crap. "Jaimie, what's happening?"

A deep male voice said, "Jaimie, please close the door."

"Sorry, Dad." Jaimie pulled Casey inside. "Casey, these are my parents."

The couple held each other as though such support kept them upright.

Casey jolted with recognition. *The couple from the campus pathway last night. The ones pursued by that bloated corpse.*

A chill shook her, and her stomach lurched. *Where's Jaimie's brother?* The pale-haired corpse swam through her thoughts. *Do I want to know?*

Jaimie's mom extended a hand. "Thank you for coming. Jaimie's told us so much about you."

Casey's voice quavered, "Sure."

Jaimie squeezed her hand, an ominous pressure that left Casey queasy.

Her father rested a heavy hand on Jaimie's shoulder. "I imagine you have a lot to talk about, so we're going to give you a few minutes. We'll be downstairs at the bar if you need us."

"Okay." Nothing animated Jaimie's voice.

She's so pale.

Jaimie stared at the closed door, hands still in her lap.

She always fidgets. Especially since the Equinox ceremony.

"Jaimie, are you okay?" *Should I hug her? Hold her hand?* Casey pulled a chair from the hotel desk and sat beside her friend.

I want to help, but what should I do?

Jaime remained stiff as a statue.

This immobility is unnatural.

Both girls jumped as the door slammed behind Jaimie's parents.

Jaimie slumped onto the bed, her eyes feverish. "My brother's missing. He disappeared after they got here. Wouldn't talk to me." Her pitch grew. Tears renewed. "Looked at me and ran."

She dissolved, inconsolable.

"Screamed something about dogs getting him."

Casey knelt before her friend. "Did you call the police?"

"Yes, of course."

"I bet they'll find him." Casey's stomach churned with the lie.

Jaimie wailed. "They came here because of me. Mom said James wouldn't sleep, kept repeating my name. He started rocking and hitting himself on the head again. He hasn't done that in years. It's like he backslid to before his years of treatment."

"What kind of treatment?"

"For his autism. They changed his diet, upped his vitamins. He took weekly socialization classes at this specialized facility. Music and art therapy, too. He was doing better. Really, he was." Jaimie blew her nose. Her voice reverberated like a stone skipped across a pond. "I know something terrible happened to him. I can feel it."

Casey stroked her friend's knotted hair. She froze. *Same color as the guy who followed the couple that night, the bloated guy spewing water.* Her knees shook. *Oh, dear Lord! The couple was Jaimie's parents. That means the guy was...*

Casey ran to the restroom and vomited.

Chapter Twenty Five

Terrible News

She left the restroom, ghost-pale and weak. She sat beside Jaimie and took her hand. *So still.* With a sidelong glance, she cleared her throat. "Jaimie, please call the police."

Jaimie moved as though weighted by deep water. "Why?"

Casey swallowed hard. She studied her hands. "I think they'll find your brother near water."

Jaimie's haunted, hollowed face turned to her. "Water? Like the lake?"

Casey felt a truth to the thought. Her lower lip trembled. She nodded.

Jaimie dialed. In a mechanical voice, she explained. "My brother is missing. My parents reported. Please check the lake. He has autism and likes water." Her eyes welled.

Two solemn police officers knocked, hats in hands.

Jaimie did not blink. Did not move. "We need to get my parents."

Casey invited the officers into the hotel room. "Please wait. Jaimie, are you okay? Do you want me to get them?"

Jaimie turned to her with haunted stillness. "Please."

"I'll get them." Casey stumbled in her rush. "I'll hurry."

She ran to the elevator. When it did not come fast enough, she pressed the button again. And again.

At last, it arrived. She pressed lobby and texted Tim. "Something bad is happening, At hotel with Jaimie and her family. Can't come to dinner. Sorry."

Before the elevator doors opened, she texted again, "I'm scared. I think her brother's dead."

No, I know he is. She rushed the door and found Jaimie's parents. She whispered, "I'm sorry to interrupt. The police are upstairs with Jaimie."

On the way to the room, Tim responded. "What can I do? Does Jaimie want me to come? Do you need me?"

The police bobbed their heads when Casey returned with Jaimie's parents. The family clutched one another. All eyes turned to the police. The environment within the hotel grew thick with apprehension.

"Sir, Ma'am, Miss." the stockier of the police officers began. "I'm terribly sorry. Campus security found a young man's body floating in the lake. They suspect an accidental drowning. The description matches the report you filed."

Jaimie shoved her fist into her mouth to block a strangled cry. Her mother's knees gave out. She slid to the bed. Her father enfolded them within his arms.

The family's grief washed over Casey, palpable and overwhelming. She quivered. Silent tears slid unchecked over Casey's cheeks.

The officer cleared his throat. "When you're able, someone needs to identify the body." He handed Jaimie's father a business card. The morgue.

Jaimie pulled her knees to her chest. Sobs wracked her.

Her mother clung. "I'll go."

Jaimie's father froze. "No. Sweetheart, I'll go."

Jaimie's mouth fell slack. "No, Mom."

Her mother stood. "If they found my baby boy, I need to see him."

Jaimie wiped her reddened face. "Me, too."

Her father's Adam's apple quivered. "We'll all go, then."

Jaimie fixed Casey with a glare.

Casey froze. *Uh oh.*

"I'll be right back." Jaimie pulled Casey into the restroom. Her reddened eyes bored into Casey's.

Casey studied the tile.

Jaimie's fingers dug into Casey. "Look at me."

Casey complied and tears poured. "How'd you know?" The words smacked of accusation to Casey's guilt-filled heart. She spluttered an incoherent response.

"Was it another vision?"

Casey sobbed. "I'm not sure. Maybe. I'm so sorry, Jaimie. So sorry." Casey buried her face in her hands.

Jaimie left Casey in her huddle of misery and joined her parents.

Her mother said, "Honey, I don't think you should go. Please stay with your friend."

"Your Mom's right. Stay here. We'll go with the police."

"I'm coming." Jaimie sniffed. "Casey'll wait for us. Won't you, Case?"

Casey ran a hand towel over her face and answered. "I'll stay as long as you need, Jaimie." A thought popped in. "Oh, Tim's worried about you. Wants to come by if he'll be of help."

Jaimie's lip quivered. "Sure. See you when we get back."

When the door latched behind them, Casey shivered. *My poor friend.*

She texted Tim, Rachel, Dad, and Aunt Hettie. "My friend's brother drowned. Can't leave her."

A knock at the door made her jump. She peered through the peephole. *Tim.* She threw open the door and collapsed into his embrace. He held her until her tears dried.

When Jaimie and her parents returned, they said little short of "Nice to meet you, Tim."

Her parents walked with stiff deliberation. Jaimie moved in uncontrollable twitches, as though the shock of seeing her twin sent her into a strange, waking hibernation.

Jaimie's mom suggested they needed to preserve their energy. "Where can we eat?"

They chose the nearby Yankee Diner. Clean, quiet, and light in patronage. They ate with mechanical movements. Casey struggled to swallow tasteless food.

I feel helpless. I hate this.

Jaimie broke the monotony of chewing. "He always loved water."

Her mother and father blinked tears silvery in the low light. Her mother wiped her eyes. "We always warned him to stay away, but it was like water called him." She sniffed. "It always drew you, too, but you've always known how to handle yourself. Like an otter."

She smiled at Jaimie. "He never understood dangers."

Jaimie buried her face in her napkin. Between sobs she whispered. "I know."

Casey placed a hand on Jaimie's shoulder. Jaimie collapsed into a heap into her embrace. Her tears soaked Casey's blouse. She hiccupped and blew her nose. Jaimie apologized with a wavery smile. "Why'd he run off, do you think? What scared him?"

Her father said, "He screamed about a big dog, but I didn't see anything." He ran a shaking hand through his gray hair. "Couldn't catch him." His chin trembled. "I tried."

"I know, Daddy. You tried. We all did. I don't understand how he got away so fast, or what spooked him. I didn't see any dogs either, but he was terrified."

Her mother studied the stitches on her sleeve. "He's been antsy like that for about a month now. Nothing we could say reached him. He started those self-soothing stim behaviors. We expected that at first, when you went away, but he seemed to have adjusted. I mean, you've been gone since summer, but recently he was inconsolable. Said something happened to his Jay-Jay."

Tim cleared his throat, eyes shifting, but said nothing.

Jaimie's mother continued, "I don't know what set him off, but since mid-September, his actions became uncontrollable, and his backsliding scared us." Tears bubbled over her red-rimmed eyes.

Her voice pitched higher. "We thought if he could see you, know you're okay, he'd calm down." Her husband pulled her into an embrace.

"He refused talking to you on the phone, so we thought driving here would work." He wiped his sleeve across his puffy eyes. "Instead, we made it worse. We lost him."

Casey pushed food around her plate and prayed for something to say to ease their grief. *Everything I can think of sounds stupid or unfeeling.* A glance at Tim's care-wrinkled forehead and soulful eyes told he shared her burden.

After dinner, Tim embraced Jaimie. "Please let me know if there is anything I can do to be of help to you." He shook everyone's hands and repeated himself as though there was nothing else he could think to say.

Jaimie's father clapped him on the back. "Thanks. You've been great." Casey walked him to his car.

Tim rubbed his brow. "How can they say I've been great? I haven't done anything of help."

She leaned her forehead against his chest. "I feel the same way."

He rested his chin on her head. His arms snaked around her like armor. "Yeah, but at least you're staying with them. Jaimie will need to talk, so you'll be more help than you realize."

Casey had rearranged her schedule to support Jaimie as best she could. She called off work, and Aunt Hettie promised to care for Rachel and Malcolm during her absence. "I can't imagine what she must be feeling. If I lost Tommy..."

Casey's throat clenched. "I know."

Tim folded himself over her and enveloped her in the shield of his embrace. She relaxed into his protection and said, "You met my kid sister and brother."

"Yeah. I like them. Cute kids."

Casey's throat worked around a secret and willed it to dislodge. "I have a brother, too. Robert. He's named for my dad. He's older than me, but we never see him. Not anymore. When my mom went crazy—" She gulped and forced the disclosure free in a whisper. "My mom's very ill, Tim. Like certifiably insane. And nobody in my family does anything about it."

Tim's steely arms drew her closer.

"Well, Robbie left. Guess Mom was too much for him to deal with, so to heck with the rest of us." Casey blinked suppressed tears. "He's been gone about six years now."

Her shoulders shook. "I'm not sure why I told you. I guess because it was like he died. Robbie, I mean. But he didn't. He chose to leave, chooses to stay away. So it's not like Jaimie's brother. It hurt worse than anything. Even worse than Mom's most evil antics."

The words caught, and she forced them out. "And Robbie's not dead. Poor Jaimie. That's her brother, her twin, and he's dead."

Tim held her until she had no more tears. He lifted her chin and stared into her eyes. "You are amazing, Casey."

Locked in his gaze, grief melted. His muscular arms warmed the shocked chill. A headache's buzz quieted.

With exaggerated care, Tim bent and pressed his lips to hers. The sensation shocked and thrilled her. *A kiss. A first kiss.*

When he stepped back, his eyes shone.

She blinked back her desire. *If only we could stay safe in each other's arms all night.*

He ran a finger along her cheek. "I won't keep you from Jaimie but call me if you need me."

Casey licked lips still tingling with reaction. *Don't trust my voice.* She nodded.

Her lips tingled long after he'd left and she'd returned to Jaimie and her grieving family.

Chapter Twenty Six

Final Arrangements

"I'm so glad you're staying with me." Jaimie grabbed Casey's hand in a hug as they walked the driveway to her family home. A tire swing hung from a thick branch of a maple tree in their front yard. Photos lined the entry of the white-sided split level captured James and Jaimie with time-capsule grace.

Jaimie made space for Casey to sit on her bed. Golden trophies ringed the room on suspended wooden shelves. When Casey asked about them, Jaimie shrugged. "I guess I was a pretty good swimmer back in the day." She patted her jiggling knees. "Wish there was an indoor pool nearby. Sure could use a dip."

They talked late into the evening. "James followed me, like, everywhere. He didn't bother me, but some of my friends thought he was creepy." She wiped tears. "He'd never harm another living being, though. Not even bugs." She chuckled, and her tears dripped from her curly lashes. "He used to call me Skeeter, like Water Skeeter, because I liked to swim so much." She clutched her knees to her chest and rocked. "He was a great person and my best friend."

She clasped Casey's hand. "Except for you."

Jaimie's grief-bloated features resembled a phantom Casey feared to acknowledge. "You're the best friend I've ever had, too, Jaimie. I'm so sorry about your brother."

Casey held Jaimie until she cried herself to sleep before curling up herself.

That night, Casey dreamed.

Devon dropped a paper at her feet. When she threw it away, the front page featured the Miss Casey Spider meme. Devon leaned over, dripping blood from his lacerated throat onto Casey's black-and-white image.

"Not bad, Casey. I think I got the likeness pretty darned well, don't you?" He used his blood to trace a heart around the picture. Casey recoiled and asked, "You?"

Devon grinned. A hulking black dog with human hands leapt from behind him and wrapped a garrote around Devon's neck, pulling deeper into the cut, exposing glints of bone. Casey screamed. Jaimie's brother ran by, flapping his hands. The dog dropped Devon to the sidewalk and pursued James. Devon reached bloody fingers to touch Casey's cheek. "You cried for me. Thank you."

Casey startled, leapt from the bed, and ran to the restroom to retch.

At breakfast, everyone pushed scrambled eggs around their plates. Nobody ate.

Jaimie's mother cleared dishes. "The director for the Huntsman Funeral Home is expecting us at ten."

"I'm coming," Jaimie's pale countenance could have been chiseled from marble, a funerary memorial to a beloved brother.

Her parents blinked, slow and sad, but said, "Okay."

Jaimie grabbed Casey's hand. "Can Casey come, too?"

Casey's heart lurched. *Shoot, what the heck am I going to do there?*

A quick study of Jaimie's needy face secured the answer. *Whatever she needs. That's what I'll do.* Casey packed tissues in her jacket pocket. *Just hope I know what she needs.*

Inside the funeral home cloyed. Mr. Huntsman, dressed in smart, somber tones, guided the family through the arrangements.

Mr. Huntsman directed them into an already set-up parlor. "This is an example of a classic display."

Flowers flanked the casket. Their heady perfume competed with stale smoke and a chemical cleanser. A lit board just inside the doorway displayed a photograph of the deceased's youth. A table opposite held a box for cards and a registry book.

A velvet kneeler allowed visitors to pray when they said their last goodbyes.

While Jaimie and her family discussed James with Mr. Huntsman, Casey perused the room. She dreaded the casket. *What if I go hysterical again, like with the ice cream family?*

But when she looked at the still corpse in her final repose, Casey felt normal sadness. *Wonder why I'm not overwhelmed like before?* She shuddered as she recalled her debilitation. *But I'm okay. Not choking on grief. Strange.* The middle-aged woman on display appeared waxen. *Maybe it's because her spirit's already gone?*

"The viewing will be closed casket." Jaimie's mother held out a pile of photos. "But these should be set up as a collage."

A glance confirmed what Casey dreaded. *He's definitely the guy I saw that night. The one with the blue lips spitting water.* Casey turned away, afraid James' smiles might transform into her water-logged vision from the other night.

Jaimie clung to her hand every chance she could. "I can't thank you enough for being here. You really are the best friend I've ever had."

She squeezed Jaimie's hand. *I wish I could do something to make this better.*

From the powder room, Casey texted Tim details for the viewing and funeral.

"Any luck getting Ryan to come? I think it would mean a lot to Jaimie."

"Sorry, Casey. He isn't coming."

"Why not?"

"Said he can't leave his art."

What a jerk. "It wouldn't be for that long, though."

"I know. I told him. Said I'd give him a ride. I'm sorry."

"It's not your fault. Thanks for asking. You'll be here though, right?"

"Yeah. I'm bringing Tommy and Red."

"Still no word on Rom?"

"Not a peep. He's not attending classes any more either. I'm worried, so I filed a report with the administration. Told them he's missing."

"What did they say?"

"Just took the information."

Casey's belly flipped about inside her. "Hope he's okay."

"He's a tough old cur. I think he'll be okay."

Casey bunked on the couch at Jaimie's house, but by turns they talked or sat in silence. Just before sunrise, Jaimie dozed off. *Guess the insomnia can come in handy at times like this.*

She pulled a crocheted blanket over Jaimie's shoulders when her friend snoozed. *Rachel said I cry and scream when I sleep. After that awful dream last night, I'm not ready to face another...* She pinched her cheeks and read curriculum books to keep sleep at bay. *Not here.*

She stole a glance at the framed family photographs. *That poor guy. My dear friend. To lose a brother. It's even worse, though. Jaimie lost a twin.* Casey clutched her pillow to muffle sound as she wept.

The funeral attendees waffled between stunned silences and discussions of unrealized potential. Although quiet, Jaimie remained active.

Casey followed her friend's agitated movements and enforced activity.

Jaimie cut through the crowds with purpose. "I can't stand by while another person thumps me on the back or tells me how sorry they are," she confided to Casey as they straightened a display of photos.

I think that's a good sign she's moving again. The stillness seemed unnatural.

Tim stood behind Casey, stiff as a sentry. *Sure is nice to have him here.*

Tommy and Red muttered condolences before they blended in with the other attendees. They returned for the funeral the next day as well.

After a solemn wake at Jaimie's casserole-filled home, they packed for their return to the campus.

When the time to leave arrived, Jaimie's parents clung to their girl.

Her father leveled a solemn appraisal over his spectacles at both Jaimie and Casey. "Please be careful. The papers report several missing people at your school. Young girls mostly, but the press reported a young man was found outside the campus last night."

Casey's stomach jolted. *Death again.* Dread made her voice quake. "Was it Devon Dare? Was his throat cut?" Casey steadied herself against the door frame. *Death on and off campus.*

He adjusted his glasses. "Yes, I think that was his name. Dare. A freshman." He nodded, a perplexed pale to his face. "Did you know him?"

Jaimie paled. "He was in a couple of our classes."

Her father clapped Jaimie's back and drew her in for a final, tight hug. "We couldn't live if something happened to you, too."

He and his wife clung to each other as they waved goodbye. *I believe that's true. I don't think they'd survive another child's death.* The girls followed Tim's van to campus. He carried Jaimie's things to her dorm room while she trapped Casey in a hug. "Thank you, Casey. You're the best friend I've ever had."

Casey's tears dampened her shoulder. "You're my best friend, too, Jaimie."

She studied Jaimie's features. "Are you okay?"

Jaimie wiped tears from swollen and reddened eyes and nodded. "Yeah, or I will be." She scanned the area before she leaned close to whisper, "How did you know that Devon Dare was killed?"

Nauseated and light-headed at the remembrance, Casey dithered.

Jaimie's eyes sparkled in the sunlight like waves, tears a tempest beneath their surface. "I thought so. You saw him." She crushed Casey's chin in another hug. "I'm so sorry. I can't imagine." She trailed off. Her mouth worked like a fish out of water.

Casey rubbed her elbow. "It will be okay. Somehow, we'll work this out."

Worry furrowed her features, but she nodded. "Yeah." She spread a strained smile. "See you soon. Tell your kid brother and sister I said hello."

Tim joined them. "Your bags are on your bed, Jaimie. The R.A. gave me a heck of time, though. She's tough, huh?"

"She sure is. Don't think any serial killer will get past her." Jaimie hugged them. "Thanks for everything, both of you." Tears glistened as she waved goodbye. The dorm door locked shut.

Tim pulled Casey to him, and she melted into his comfort.

Wish I could stay here forever.

He stepped back, a hungry expression in his eyes. "You have to go." His Adam's apple worked overtime. "I'll walk you to your car, and you have to promise to be extra careful." He cupped her chin and Casey searched his intense gaze. "I'm serious."

She nodded. "You, too. It's not only ladies who are being killed." *Like Devon. And maybe James.* A lump rose in her throat. *Like James? Why'd I think that? Could the killer have killed him, too?* "I don't want anything bad to happen to you." She squeezed his hands and marveled at their solid strength.

He squeezed back. "Only good things for us." He leaned forward and kissed her.

She closed her eyes. His lips massaged hers. Tingling tracks. Tongues searched. Promised. Probed. She quivered. *Oh my gosh, don't stop kissing me.* His arms tightened around her, pulled her to his warmth. Like a safe port in a storm.

She rested her cheek against his chest. He ran a strand of her hair through his fingers. She shivered.

His voice husky and breathless. "I'm so glad I met you, Casey." His eyes sparkled.

They held hands and kissed goodbyes. And kissed again. And again, until at last Casey sighed. "I have to get home."

Heat from his touch lingered Casey's entire trip home.

Rachel greeted Casey at the door with wide-eyes and trembling lips. She whispered, "Aunt Hettie's here." The girls crept toward the staircase but paused when their mother's voice rose in agitation.

"Look here, Hettie, I can't just leave. Did you forget I'm sick?"

Hettie exuded calm, from her Zen-like posture to her half-closed eyes. She kept her tone monotonous as a metronome, and she moved her hands like a willow tree in the wind. Through such gentle measures, Aunt Hettie sometimes helped Mom see reason. "Marlin's our nephew, and he just lost his mom. He's just a kid. Our brother needs our help because I don't think he's dealing with his wife's death well."

Aunt Mae died? Casey and Rachel locked frightened stares. *She was younger than Mom and Aunt Hettie.*

Mom growled like a big cat. "How's any of that my problem?"

Hettie sighed. "Like I said, sometimes helping others has a way of helping us as well." She leaned forward. "Come on, sis. It'll only be a couple of days."

She touched Mom's leg with her finger-tips, her eyes hopeful as a puppy's. "We might be able to do some good."

Mom recoiled. "There's no way I can leave."

She rested her elbows on the back of the couch. "Look, I appreciated your help while Casey went skipping about doing whatever she does, but I'm needed here. Even if she makes it home, I can't rely on her. Can't really rely on anyone. Besides, I told you before. I'm too sick to travel."

Heat rose in Casey's cheeks. *Can't rely on me? Skipping about?*

"All right." Hettie shuffled about the room to gather her jacket and gloves. "I really hoped you'd come."

Hettie planted a kiss on her sister's forehead. "Be nice to the kids while I'm gone, will ya? You've got the best family I know."

"Yeah, yeah, that's only because you don't have to live with them."

Hettie's keys jingled in her grip. "You have no idea how blessed you are." She headed to the door. "Tell them I said goodbye, and I'll see them soon. I love you, sis."

Mom never answered. She curled up on the couch and fell asleep.

Chapter Twenty Seven

Happy Halloween

The end of October brought frost on jack-o-lanterns and gluts of candy on store shelves.

Tim walked Casey to class. They shuffled leaves beneath their feet, hands clasped.

"Are you taking your sis and little bro trick-or-treating?"

"Yeah. Rachel's going as a wizard student. You'll never guess Malcolm's costume. He's a superhero."

He laughed. "Never saw that coming. When are you going??"

"Trick-or-treating is on Friday this year."

"Until 8?"

"Yeah. Why?"

"Well, I was thinking. We keep trying to get together for this date, and it ends up being a group thing every time. Don't misunderstand. I don't mind. I'd do whatever it takes to spend time with you."

She blushed.

I feel the same way.

"Here's my thought. Let's embrace the circumstances and seize the latest opportunity. I'll come trick-or-treating with you and the kids, if that's okay.

"Then you come to the school Halloween dance with me after. The dance starts at dusk, but it runs late. It's costumed. 'Stages of Grief' was supposed to play for it, but I think the band's done. Nobody comes to practice any more except Red, and she's been acting weird. Real distant. Ryan won't leave his room, Tommy's obsessed with Native American stuff, and Rom's still missing."

"No word on where he is?"

"Nope. His car's gone, and he's still not been to classes."

"Have you talked to his folks?"

"Yeah. They haven't heard from Rom in a long time. No clue where he might be."

Her stomach jolted. "I hope he's okay."

"Me, too."

Casey pushed aside her disquiet about Rom. "Let's make your plan work. I'll take the kids out right after dinner. Maybe you can meet me in the neighborhood. After, we'll go to the school party. What are you going to dress up like?"

"I'm not sure. My roommate has these ren faire clothes that he said I could borrow."

"Like kings and stuff?"

"Yeah. Maybe you could dress up like a queen."

She squirmed. "Matching costumes seems awfully couple-y, doesn't it?"

He snatched her hand and kissed it. "I hope we are couple-y."

He always makes me blush. "I'll see what I can come up with."

After class, Casey brought Jaimie a pumpkin spice latte. Jaime studied by the lake, wrapped in layers atop a picnic table. Chilled breezes pulsed from the water. Casey blew on her hands. "Jaimie, maybe we should go inside. It's getting cold. I can't feel my nose anymore."

Jaimie shrugged and nestled further under a school stadium blanket. "You don't have to stay with me."

Casey sighed. "Scooch over, girlfriend, and share those blankets." *It's not so bad.* "So, Tim asked if I'd like to go to a costume party on Friday. I'm taking the kids trick-or-treating, so we'll go after. You're coming, right?"

"Don't think so. Being a third wheel isn't my thing."

"We're going to ask Red, too, and there will be lots of kids from school there. Besides, you're never a third wheel. You're our friend, and—"

She grabbed Jaimie's hand. "—you're my best friend."

"Thanks. About that. Would you still be my friend if I were different?"

"Different how?"

She studied the undulations of the lake's waters. "I don't know. I feel like the me I was keeps drifting away."

Casey threw her arms around her friend. Jaimie. Jaimie shook. *Life is full of ironic circles. This is like when I first met Jaimie, and she pulled me out of my shell.* "I'll always be your friend, no matter where you drift."

Jaimie stared as waves lapped over the lake's shore. "Thanks, Casey. You're the best."

At home, Casey adapted an old dress from the attic. *I think this was Aunt Hettie's prom dress.*

Mothballs and cedar chest smells permeated the material. Assessing herself in the cheval mirror in the bathroom, she decided. "It'll do." She squirted it with cologne.

Rachel squealed. "You look wonderful! Oh, I know! We should braid pearls into your hair. I watched a tutorial on-line."

Casey endured her tugs and enjoyed her prattle.

"Someday, I'm going to Savini's school and learn how to do FX and beauty makeup and make appliances.

"Bonnie in my class is allowed to wear makeup. Mom would flip out if I wore makeup, don't you think?"

Casey nodded. "You're stunning without makeup, sweet-pea."

Rachel pulled the hair from the nape of Casey's neck and twisted it into a crown. "That's such a big sister thing to say. Everyone can use a bit of a pick me up. Here, let me put on your lipstick. I know how to accent your lips with an alternating color. See?"

Her application gave Casey's lips a playful pout. "Nice!"

Rachel shrugged. "It's what I do during study hall. Watch instructional videos and practice with Bonnie's makeup." She fingered a compact pallet of eyeshadows from Casey's bag.

"For instance, you can change the way a person looks with contour shading. Watch." She used a charcoal to hollow out Casey's cheek bones and brightened the apples with a pale salmon.

"Wow, that's really cool! Great job, kid!"

Rachel sighed. "I can't wait until I can wear makeup."

She's growing up too fast. Casey slipped an eyeliner, the shadow, and some powder into her wristlet.

"Before you know it, you'll be all grown and will be able to wear any makeup you want. Time to get dressed, though, or you'll miss trick or treats."

Rachel burst from the room. "Be back. Malcolm, get your costume on!"

Malcolm called, "It's already on."

Casey laughed. "Can't really trick or treat when you're all grown up and wearing makeup, by the way."

The kids grabbed their pillow cases and flashlights. "Let's go!"

Casey snapped a photo of the kids with her phone and then called to Mom. "We're heading out." She hunched down to the kids. "Give Mom a kiss before we go."

Malcolm ran to comply. Rachel crossed her arms and thrust out her chin.

Casey asked, "What's going on, Rachel?"

"Just don't see why she doesn't come out here to see us. We treat her like she's some sort of Rajah."

"She's sick, Rach. She can't help it."

"That's what everyone says. When's she going to get better?"

Good question. "I don't know the answer to that, but I think she's trying."

But is she? Is she trying to be well?

Casey's head hummed with premonition.

Rachel's cheeks blazed. "She's mean, Casey."

Casey kissed the top of her sister's head.

"I'm sorry. We have to be patient."

Rachel stomped into the living room, pirouetted, and returned to the foyer. She ignored her mother's calls for a hug from her 'precious girl.' "Can we go now? I want candy, and daylight's a-wasting."

They met Tim at the assigned corner. Dressed in a suit of armor, he dazzled.

"Oooh," Rachel gasped.

You're not kidding, little sis. Casey curtseyed, blushed, and giggled. "Sir knight, have you come to rescue us?"

He bowed from the waist, the metal creaked. "At your service, beautiful ladies." He bowed a second time toward Malcolm. "Excellent sir." He cradled Casey's hand in his metal gauntlet and kissed like a gallant gentleman.

Casey and Rachel gasped. Casey's hand warmed where his lips lingered. The heat in her cheeks intensified.

Malcolm's face twisted in disgust. "Yuck!"

They laughed and set off along the sidewalk. Crisp air sent swirls of decayed leaves.

The neighbors went all-out with decorations. With its bubbling cauldron and canned cackles, the Sanderson house gave them the happy creeps. Billy Butcherson set up a graveyard where dry-ice fog rolled among the Styrofoam tombstones.

Several neighbors set bonfires ablaze, huddled near its warmth, and gave treats to the children.

Casey reminded them, "Don't forget to say thank you."

Their voices dutifully sing-songed the "Trick or Treat" and "Thank you!"

Malcolm dragged his pillow case behind him.

Rachel scowled. "Pick that up, Malcolm. If you wear a hole it that, Mom'll kill us."

Malcolm whined, "It's too heavy."

Tim bowed, his metal creaking. "May I be of service, my good sir?" He hefted the bag over his shoulder like an armored St. Nick. "This is heavy! Maybe I should carry yours, too, Rachel?"

Rachel giggled and twirled her hair as she handed the bag to him. "Thanks, Tim. I thought my shoulder was going to break."

They waved to firefighters and police who patrolled the neighborhood.

Rachel giggled when a younger volunteer fireman handed them glow sticks. "You kids be safe."

They snapped and hung the sticks around the kids' necks. Tim said, "Seem like there are more safety patrols this year."

Casey nodded and watched the red of the fire truck's lights flash over the kids. She whispered, "Guess a murderer on campus not too many miles away will make a town a bit jumpy."

Tim squeezed her shoulder.

One house boasted a mad scientist's laboratory. The homeowner blasted "Iron Maiden" and took swigs from a tankard as he doled out handfuls of candy.

A black cat twined around their legs at the Dennison's, to Rachel's delight. She squealed and bent to pet the purring creature. "I wish I could take you home and make you mine!"

Casey frowned. Their mother would never allow them a pet. "They're dirty," she'd complain as she'd drop a crumpled bag of consumed chips to a pile on the floor near her post in the living room.

Once Mother fell asleep, Casey and the kids would clean up their mother's messes.

But we can't have a pet because we wouldn't know how to clean up after them.

Casey shook off the thoughts when Tim brushed a fallen leaf from her hair. He leaned in and whispered, "I'm having a lot of fun. Thanks for inviting me."

Warmth filled Casey. "We're glad you came, too."

Malcolm stomped over and placed his hands on his hips. "By the way, Tim, don't forget that's our candy. You can't just take it."

Although Tim's lips trembled with suppressed laughter, his tone remained respectful. "Of course, Sir Malcolm. I'd never dream of pilfering your loot."

Malcolm's face crunched into lines of confusion. "Pilfering our loot?"

Casey scooped him into her arms. "That means steal your candy, silly!"

Malcolm kicked. "Put me down! I'm a super-hero, Casey, not a little brother."

"Oh, I'd forgotten." She kissed his head, and he rushed to join Rachel at the next porch.

Laden with treats, the group returned home. They stopped before entering the driveway.

Rachel considered Tim from the corner of her eyes. "Are you two coming in? I'll share my candy."

Casey flipped the hood of her sister's wizard robe over her head. "We need to get going, or we'll miss the whole party at school. Jaimie and Red are waiting for us, and it would be rude to be late."

Rachel scowled but nodded. Casey hugged her siblings.

"Be sure the candy's checked before you eat any, okay? Daddy will be home soon, and Aunt Hettie said she'd stop over after work."

"All right. I love you, Casey." Rachel hugged her again and turned to Tim. She chewed her lip.

"Thanks for coming with us, Tim. Happy Halloween."

Tim clanked as he bowed. "It was my pleasure, Lady Wizard, Sir Superhero. Happy All Hallows' Eve to you both."

Rachel cocked her head with an impish smile. "By the way, please wish your brother Tommy a Happy Halloween for me."

Casey closed her eyes and shook her head, but Tim nodded. "Of course."

They waited until the kids blinked the porch light to indicate they were inside safe and sound before they walked to Tim's car. He drove them to NorEast campus, metal knees clanking as he braked.

Casey asked, "Is it hard to drive in that get-up?"

He turned his head stiffly around the leather and steel gorget. "A little." He cleared his throat. "By the way, did you hear about Devon Dare? They found him dead off campus."

Devon with his throat shredded, pouring blood onto his goofy t-shirt.

Tim touched her knee. "You okay? You look like you're going to be sick."

"How'd he die? Do you know?"

"Police said it was wild dogs. Animal control's been rounding up strays and euthanizing them."

Jaimie waited on the bench outside of her dorm. Moonlight her spotlight, Jaimie resembled a mythical actress center stage. She stood, shook loose her curls, and shimmied over to greet them. Layers of luminous fabric hugged her hips, a sexy mermaid tail that impeded her movement.

Sheer material gave the illusion of an exposed midriff, and fabric shells covered her personal bits.

Casey gasped. "Wow, you look great!"

"Thanks. So do you."

As they walked to the party, Jaimie said, "I'm glad you're here. Security came by twice. They've been talking about instating a curfew since the latest disappearance."

Two men in gorilla suits guarded the door. Music pounded within. Casey paused. *I hate crowds and loud music.* Tim wrapped an arm around her shoulders. She buckled a bit beneath the armor's weight.

"By the way," Jaimie said, "I visited Ryan today."

She studied the nearest gorilla's fur. "Thought he might join us."

Tim said, "I'm guessing since he's not here, he wasn't interested." He mumbled, "The idiot."

Jaimie shook her head. "No. He's too busy with his art." Her voice broke. "You should see the place. Canvases everywhere. The place smells like turpentine, enough to make you high. You'll never guess who he's painting."

Casey knew. "Her."

"Yep. Her. Red hair in a dark woods, White hair peeking from behind marble pillars. A blonde dropping a hankie from a castle tower. Silvery, singing to the moon. Chestnut, ebony, black.

"But always Her. She looks different, but it's Her. You can tell by the eyes and expression."

She swallowed and lowered her voice. "I asked if he was in love with her. He said, 'Of course. She's my muse. She's every heroine. Helen, Juliette, Isolde, Cleopatra. She is the ideal and the well-spring.' Then he told me to get out that I disrupted his art." She wiped tears from her lashes. "He's going to fail out of school, you know. He's not been to class since that night in the woods."

"I'm sorry, Jaimie," Tim and Casey said, almost in unison.

She shrugged. "Let's get inside. It's cold out here, and I'm not exactly dressed for the elements. Besides, isn't Red meeting us inside?"

They nodded. Casey's stomach lurched and churned like a tempest-besieged sea. *I don't want to go in there.* Still, she followed her friends.

Chapter Twenty Eight

All Hail Samhain

They walked passed the gorilla guards and entered a vast marble hall. Music echoed. Doorways to the entertainment complex branched from the hallway. Laughter and rock music to the right overpowered pop music played in a bar with hors d'oeuvres to the left. Casey gripped Tim's and Jaimie's arms, the air too thick to breath.

Jaimie said, "Do you need a minute?"

Casey nodded and wiped sweat from her hairline.

Tim's brows knitted together as he resumed his sentry-type posture. His hand rested on her shoulder.

She leaned into his strength.

"Ms. Adams, what a pleasant surprise." Dr. Bridges stepped with the assurance of tenure toward them. "My, what interesting costumes." His eyes twinkled as he took in their attire. "Do you know, there is a theory that the costumes chosen to celebrate All Hallows' Eve reflect an aspect of the wearer's personality. If that is the case, you three are perfectly matched." He continued to assess their get ups.

Seeing Dr. Bridges surprised her. "Thank you, I think." His tailored suit and wing-tip shoes seemed out of place. "Where's your costume?"

"Just passing through, but when I saw you all here, it seemed prudent to stop." He tilted his head, staring at her. "Ms. Adams, are you well?"

I hate crowds. I haven't slept properly in days. I'm worried about my home life, I'm worried about my friends, and I'm hoping I'm doing well with school. Not to mention money troubles. I don't want to share any of that though. She shrugged.

Jaimie squeezed her hand. "Crowds aren't really Casey's thing." They watched a group of drunken girls stumble from the bar. Red wore a Little Red Riding Hood costume. She wobbled on her stilettos and giggled.

Casey broke from Jaimie's grip and backed into a cold marble pillar. Solid, it kept her upright, though her knees threatened to collapse. A scream strangled within her throat.

No! Rooted and unable to run, she couldn't blink, couldn't look away. Tears burned her cheeks.

Why can't I look away?

Blood darkened Red's hair. It dripped from the waves to leave a ruby trail.

Slashes crisscrossed her sexy pinafore and holes riddled her fishnet stockings.

Red's dancer legs missed chunks. Bloodied bone, shredded muscles, and ragged tendons glistened. Claw marks marred the side of her face.

Red scowled at Casey. "What's wrong with her?" Blood and teeth gushed and splattered with each word.

Dr. Bridges said, "Somebody, catch her. She looks like she's going to faint."

I wish I could. Words strangled within her. Thoughts came out in apoplectic pops. Red's color drained with each rattled breath. *It's not makeup. Gosh, I wish it were makeup.*

Jaimie and Tim closed in, concern distorted their faces. Tim slid an arm around her shoulders, and Jaimie held her hand.

Casey slid along the pillar, legs unsteady, and ran for the exit. She tripped on her gown's hem and stumbled to a bench outside. The air cooled her tears, but nothing dislodged the vision. Red, torn apart, throat eaten. Red, her beautiful voice silenced forever. Red, covered in her namesake.

Casey curled into a ball, clutched her head, and sobbed.

"Casey, are you okay?" Jaimie jittered beyond reach, as though afraid of contact.

Tim marched around her and took Casey in his arms.

The armor made his embrace hard and indelicate. *Like hugging an armadillo.* His suit reflected the light, and he shined.

"Tim, we have to save her," Casey said.

"What? Casey, I don't know what you're talking about."

"Jaimie, did you see her? Did you see Red?" Her voice bordered on hysteria.

Jaimie knelt before the bench as though in prayer, her costume pulled tight. "Casey, is it like the other day, with the family at the ice cream shop?"

Casey nodded. *You have to calm down. Pull yourself together. Red's life may depend on it.* "Tim, go get Red. She's in danger. Something terrible's going to happen to her if we don't protect her."

Tim pressed Casey closer to his chest. The armor left indents in her skin.

She pushed him. "Stop it! I'm fine. She's not. Get Red, please." Tears drenched her face. "Never mind! I'll find her myself." Casey stumbled after the macabre vision.

Tim grabbed her arm. His face twisted with desperation. "Please stay here, Casey. I'll look for Red." His blood pounded through his jugular, and he gulped. Dr. Bridges clapped his shoulder as he walked passed. The action rang like a funeral bell.

"Casey," the professor said, "Dr. Krochalis is here, too. Can we talk with you, please?"

Great. They think I'm a loon. She wiped at the tears, but new ones fell.

They approached, hands outstretched.

Guess they think I might bite. She hiccupped.

They flanked her on the bench. Dr. Krochalis spoke first. "What happened? What did you see?"

Red awash in blood. Red, her beauty mangled and disfigured. Red, glazed eyes staring from a leafy grave.

She choked on tears and hugged her knees.

Jaimie cleared her throat. "This happened one other time, right? A family at the ice cream place. Is it the same thing, Casey?"

Casey nodded, terrorized by tears and visions of death. She sobbed. *Not only one other time. Devon. And your brother. Oh God, your brother.*

A hand touched her shoulder, an attempt at comfort. Casey recoiled, but the hand remained.

Dr. Krochalis asked, "Has this always happened to you?"

No. She shook her head. *No. Who could endure this always happening?*

"When did it start?" Male voice. Dr. Bridges.

"I'm not sure," Jaimie said. "Casey?"

She croaked, "Equinox."

They shifted on the bench. The hand grew heavier. "Did you participate in the hilltop ceremony? The one run by Lily and that fellow. What's his name?"

Dr. Bridges said, "Mabon, isn't it?"

"Yes, that's his name."

Jaimie gasped.

"You know about the ceremony? We thought it was super-secret." Jaimie tapped her forehead. "That's right. You started it, didn't you, Dr. K?"

Dr. Krochalis nodded.

"Years ago, but others took it over some time ago. Lily was my student. I don't know her friend. New age fellow. Older, right? Runs a bookstore in town. I hear she works for him now. Lives with him."

Jaimie said, "Do you know the other woman? I don't remember her name." She shuddered.

Casey shivered again. "Cassandra."

Dr. Krochalis looked away and scratched the side of her head. "Cassandra? I don't think I know a Cassandra. Geof, do you?"

She's hiding something.

Dr. Bridges shook his head. His voice clear. "No. Me either."

Jaimie asked, "So, does everyone know about the ceremony?"

Dr. Krochalis said, "Not everyone, but interested parties are aware. It is an awakening ceremony at a time the world prepares for sleep. It calls to and defines the spirit."

Reveal your true natures. The balance reset.

Jaimie's voice shook. "That's kinda what they said. What did we do?"

Dr. Krochalis asked, "Are you having visions, too?"

"Not exactly. We all have dreams, though, with a witch. She's watching, calling, like she wants to use us."

Dr. Krochalis's face paled. "What's the witch like?"

"Beautiful. Dangerous. Terrifying. She stalks like a panther, disappearing and reappearing behind things. For me, it's like she's under water." Jaimie plucked at her costume. "Some of the others say she's in different places, but certain aspects are always the same. She disappears behind one object and reappears in a new place. It's like she wants to break free or something."

Dr. Krochalis and Dr. Bridges exchanged nods. She said, "If it's who I think, she's been imprisoned a long time."

"Tim's little brother has turned native. He's obsessed with Native Americans now.

"Rom's missing. Nobody knows where he is. Ryan..." Jaimie fell silent and dropped her gaze.

Dr. Krochalis ran her hand through her hair and disturbed the chin-length strands. "She looks for agents to use."

Jaimie's voice trembled. "Does she always come to the Equinox ceremony?"

Dr. Krochalis shook her head. "No. It seems weird, but I believe you're describing an ancient being. Some culture worshiped her. Maybe she's not a real person at all."

Dr. Bridges raised his eyebrows. "Many in the psychological field would call her an archetype, a manifestation of a higher calling within yourself."

Casey said through tears, "How do we stop her?"

Dr. Krochalis swallowed. "You don't."

Chapter Twenty Nine

Little Red

Gooseflesh raised along Casey's arms. "We don't?" Her voice shrilled. "We don't stop her? What do we do? Live like this?"

Dr. Krochalis shook her head, her eyes narrowed. "Not necessarily. You volunteered. By theory, you can either reject the lessons or embrace them. However, you took part in a ceremony that welcomed these changes, including the Lady's presence. It could be deemed an acceptance of the terms. Remember, responsibility for knowledge."

Casey grew silent. Tears trickled unchecked over her cheeks. Cold ran through her.

St. Thomas. Last lesson.

"But we didn't know the rules. How can we be bound to a contract if we never agreed to the terms?"

Jaimie's hand flew to cover her mouth. She shook her head and muttered, "But it's true. We didn't know. They didn't say our lives would change like this."

Casey sobbed. *They sort of did. Maybe we just didn't believe it could touch us so profoundly.*

Dr. Bridges rested a hand on her shoulder.

"Don't worry. When you know yourself, you can overcome any obstacle."

Casey asked "Does this happen to everyone when they participate? Visions and—" She fought nausea.

Dr. Bridges pressed his lips together and shook his head. "Forgive me, but this seems like unsubstantiated hysteria."

Dr. Krochalis bit her lip until it bled. "Pardon me but I think you are mistaken, Dr. Bridges. I believe this is quite real, and no. I don't think everyone has the same reaction. I think the spirit answers the call set forth during the ceremony. Our purest self, reacts."

Casey moaned. "Can I make it stop?"

Dr. Krochalis stroked her chin. "I can't answer that."

Jaimie swayed, a reed bent in breezes. "I don't think I can take this much longer. We have to find a way to put things back the way they were."

Dr. Bridges stood and offered Jaimie his seat on the bench. "Are you having visions, too?"

Her voice far-away. "Not really. Like I said, for me it's more like a pull."

Before she elaborated, Tim burst on the scene. His costume clattered and clanked. He doubled over to catch his breath. "I found her. She's with Rom."

Rom?

Jaimie said, "Wait, you found Rom?"

Tim nodded and resumed an upright stance. "Running's not easy in this get up. I didn't recognize him at first. Wild costume. Some kind of wolf man, I think. Red was going on about how their costumes were perfect for each other. Said she was glad he finally found her."

What was Red wearing? Casey's mind slid from thoughts of her friend. *Don't want to picture it. Don't want to picture her.*

"Anyway, I thought since she was safe, I'd check on you. How are you feeling, Casey?"

Casey quivered. Unbidden images seeped. *Red in a pretty, puffed sleeved shirt dripping gore. Red, her long legs jutting at odd angles beneath a short pinafore. Red, big eyes staring with accusation.*

She leapt from the bench and smacked Tim's breast plate. "No! She's not safe. Don't you understand? She's going to die." She glared through tears. "Where are they?"

"By Pugh Lecture Hall." His eyes wide and hurt. "I don't understand, Casey..."

Without explanation, Casey ran toward the Hall.

Tim clattered behind her. "Stop, Casey. Please. If there's danger-" but with a sprint, she left him behind. Urgency electrified her.

Jaimie slid into her peripheral view. She huffed, her costume torn along the seam.

"I'm with you."

No sign of Red or Rom at Pugh.

"You go that way, and I'll take this path." Jaimie took off as instructed.

Tim's metallic clanking told of his approach.

In mid-stride, pain ripped through Casey. Her scream strangled. *Red's dead. I felt her die.*

She collapsed and wailed. "No!"

Tim gathered Casey into his arms.

Chapter Thirty

Enlightened Minds

Casey bought an energy bar at the Student Union. Tim and Jaimie froze before a television screen. Jaimie grabbed Casey's arm, fingers biting. "It's Red. They found her by the willow trees. By the lake."

The newscaster smiled through the report: "... police suspect the nineteen-year-old was the victim of another animal attack."

No—no, it wasn't Casey gulped. "Rom killed her."

Jaimie paled, eyes widened. "Why would you say that?"

"Because it's true."

Tim slumped, as though kicked in the stomach. "I'm sorry, Casey." Like a hurt child, his eyes wide with fear. "Why would he? Everyone knew he loved Red."

Jaimie pointed to the newscaster. "Maybe the police are right. Stray dogs can be vicious. I've heard some of the local farmers lost a bunch of sheep, too."

I feel like a statue, cold and cried out.

Tim reached for her hand, but she folded hers in her lap.

Jaimie crumpled the paper cup she carried. Cold pumpkin spice latte streamed to her wrist.

"I don't understand where he is, though. Why can't we reach Rom?"

Because he doesn't want to be found. "Murderers need to remain hidden if they are to continue their *work*."

Jaimie twisted the paper in her hands until it formed a dual-edged sword. "Casey, stop saying that. Rom loved her."

Loved her to death.

"Still can't believe Ryan didn't come to my brother's funeral. Bet he won't come for Red, either."

Jaimie threw the paper cup into the trash with a thud. "Well, let's get out of here. Walk somewhere. Do something."

Tim sighed. "I know. Casey, do you feel like driving into town? Dr. Krochalis suggested checking out Mabon's shop. We could see if she's available to come along, if she's not busy with office hours or classes."

A wind blew from the lake, and clouds threatened snow. Dr. Krochalis' office door opened when they knocked, but the professor was not there.

Tim said, "Wonder where she is?"

Jaimie turned a notepad atop the desk blotter and touched a page with neat handwriting. She jotted a note in her own reedy scrawl. "I'll let her know we stopped by and where we're going."

Chills crept up Casey's spine as she climbed into her car with her friends. She followed the GPS directions on her phone to Mabon's shop, "Enlightened Minds."

Wind chimes sounded their entrance. Books stacked on shelves lining the walls. Tables boasted fragrant spell ingredients. An open chest of crystals resembled pirate's booty. Wands, fairy wings, animal parts, Native American crafts, masks, and statues crowded the space. Ocarina music and incense set a mood. Casey's head throbbed. *I hate incense.*

"Namaste." Mabon stepped from the back room. The full-spectrum lights cast his pouchy cheeks and bald head into stark contrasts.

He resembles the suns Malcolm draws, with ridiculous smiley faces in the center of the circle.

He reached for her hand. "Beautiful lady, welcome."

Casey evaded with folded her arms as she examined a pan pipe on the counter. *I don't think he recognizes us.*

He caught and kissed Jaimie's hand.

Yuck.

Why is something that was sweet when Tim did it turn so darned weird when this creep does it? She set aside the pipes and ran her finger along an engraved wooden flute. *Native fertility, Cochina.*

Tim pointed. "Tommy would like that, I bet."

Mabon said, "May your spirits be at peace. You've come to a place of enlightenment."

Well, that's the name of the place, isn't it? Gosh, he's annoying.

"Look around until you find what you seek."

Casey glared at the guy. "We need to talk to you."

"Oh? Well, I have consultations after seven if you'd like to make an appointment." He reached across the counter and grabbed a date book. "The required donation is fifty dollars per half hour. What time would you like to schedule your reading?"

Casey stepped away and held her breath. *Mabon's antiperspirant must have expired hours ago.*

Tim cleared his throat and wiped his nose. "No, you don't understand. We need to talk to you about the ceremony you conducted in September."

The book fell to the counter. Like dough, Mabon's face reconfigured when he drew his eyebrows together. "What about it?"

"We need you to reverse the effects."

Mabon intoned, less airy. "Reverse the effects? It doesn't work that way."

"I get that, but we're having trouble. Real trouble, and it all comes from that experience."

"Look. You participated voluntarily. I'm not responsible if you don't like the outcome."

Jaimie slapped the counter, her face a mask of conflicted emotions. "See, here's the problem. None of us sleep any more.

"I have a hard time breathing, and if I stay still, I feel like I might die. My friend has premonitions of death. People she knows and strangers. Bloody visions with gore and everything. Scary stuff, y'know? My Ryan. Well he can't stop painting." She stomped. "We're all affected."

Her voice trembled near hysteria, her eyes wide and frightening. "But worst of all, our friend Red was killed, and Casey thinks another participant in your stupid ceremony might have done it. So, we're really not just asking..."

Mabon's eyes bulged. He crossed his arms and lips pressed thin. "I can't help you. This is between you and the Creator."

Heat flashed through Casey's cheeks. Her nostrils flared, and anger electrified her. "No, it is between us and the woman, the snake, that witch who duped us into these changes. Get her. We need to talk to her now."

Mabon backed away from Casey's advance. Her held up his hands as though in surrender. "Witch? Hold on. I'll get Lily."

Casey clenched fists. "Not Lily. The other one. The tall woman who really ran things. Cassandra. We need her."

He puffed and stiffened his posture. "Cassandra? How do you even know her name? Besides, she didn't run things." He poked his chest with a plump thumb. "I organize the Equinox ceremonies. Have for the last six years."

He's a blowhard. He can't help us. She struggled to control her quavering voice. "We need Cassandra. Now, please."

He shrugged and turned his attention to a tabletop display of New Age books he authored. "Well, sorry, but I don't know how to reach her. She's not part of our circle. Just showed up and offered her help. Lily thought she knew her from some other lifetime. She was spectacular, but we haven't seen her since." His eyes unfocused as he sighed. He shook alert. "I'll get Lily, though. She might be able to help."

He waddled into the back room.

Casey gasped.

Lily entered. Translucent skin stretched over her face and left shoulder.

Lily's voice distant. "Hello, everyone. How are you?"

Tim and Jaimie offered greetings.

Casey squeezed her eyes shut, but when she opened them, Lily remained unchanged. A layer of skin hugged Lily's mouth. It vibrated with each word. In and out with her breath, it suffocated. The veil settled tighter, a sack over the head of the condemned.

No, please.

Quaking, Casey slid to the floor She stared slack-jawed at the apparition. Tears slid like oil slicks over her cheeks.

Not again.

Chapter Thirty-One

The Truth Will Out

Lily reached for Casey. "Are you all right, dear?"

No, no, no, no!

Casey cringed and closed her eyes. *No escaping Lily with the asphyxiation caul. Her eyes bulged, and her swollen tongue protruded from blue-tinted lips. She reached for Casey, and her fingernails matched her lips, darkening to purple at the nail beds. Her skin darkened to an unpleasant violet.*

The woman's grazed touch left Casey weak, and she shuffled into a table leg to escape. A rain of crystals clattered around her, like frozen tears.

A moan bubbled through Casey's trembling lips. Her tears flooded. She gasped for breath. *I can't keep doing this. I'm going crazy.*

Lily turned to Tim and Jaimie. She asked in her wispy voice, "Good heavens, really, what's wrong with her?"

Tim knelt. "Casey, honey, it's okay."

Casey searched Lily's face for hope. Instead Lily's face weakened, struggled. Within Lily's brain, just above her left temple, an eruption began.

No, it's not. Nothing is okay. She buried her face in her knees and sobbed.

Tim climbed under the table and wrapped her close to his chest. He stroked her hair. "I've got you."

Jaimie chewed her fingernails and rocked behind Lily. Her fingers fretted. "Casey," she whispered, "should I call an ambulance?"

Half of Lily's face drooped. "Yes. Hurry."

Jaimie tapped a three-digit dirge into her phone.

"What is—" Lily clutched the table. Her nails dug into the wood. She fell and knocked her head.

She scratched at her chest, gouged and pulled at her clothes. She gasped and choked. Her eyes bulged. A high-pitched wheeze whistled through her, the inevitable death rattle.

Tim pulled Casey, away from the fallen woman. "Holy God!" He kept an arm wrapped around Casey while he dialed emergency services as well. "I think she's having a heart attack or a stroke."

Jaimie yelled, "Mabon."

Blood darkened Lily's hair and pooled like a macabre halo.

Tim pushed Casey behind him. "Come quick, please. She just fell and hit her head. There's blood everywhere. Hurry!"

Jaimie ran behind the counter to the back room as Tim gave directions.

Casey's tears dripped. She crept around Tim. She reached to wipe the hair from Lily's eyes. She choked on her tears. "I'm so sorry."

Lily's skin paled and grew waxy. Her mouth formed labored, whispered words. "Thank you for mourning me."

She wheezed. "Your tears cleanse the path, leaving the way shining like silver." Her breath rattled. "What a blessing."

Casey touched the woman's decimated cheek. *I wish I could do more to help.*

The caul spread tight against Lily's chest, collected in her mouth, and clogged her breath. Lily convulsed, shuddered, and died.

While closing Lily's eyes, Casey whispered, "Rest in peace."

Careless of the blood, Casey curled into a ball and cried.

With gentle care, Tim lifted and cradled Casey as if she were a child. "The ambulance is on its way."

Casey sniffed into his shoulder. *Too late.*

Jaimie burst from the office. The door slammed. "He's gone."

So's she.

Tim's grip tightened. "Mabon? That weasel! Where'd he go?"

"I don't know. Just gone. But I found this on the floor by the back door. I wonder if he dropped it on his way out." She held a paper with an address. 699 Lakefront Drive. "Lakefront Estates are close to campus. It's where a lot of the professors live."

Tim said, "We have to wait for the ambulance, but after, if you're feeling well enough, Casey, let's check this place out."

Chapter Thirty-Two

699 Lakefront

Tim squeezed Casey's knee. "The EMT's said there wasn't much we could do to help her. Massive aneurism. Man, she wasn't that old."

She drove. *There never is anything I can do. Just cry. What good is there in that?*

They pulled into the driveway of 669 Lakefront behind three cars, a white Mercedes, a beat-up Honda, and an ill-kept black sports car. The red brick two-story house mirrored the rest of the new construction in the up-scale planned community.

The whole place is a study in sameness, a vanilla community where individuality is stomped out. Casey rubbed her temples. Each blink an agonized remembrance. She shook her head to clear it. *Can't afford thoughts of death or 'clearing the way' for the dying. Not now.* "I recognize some of the neighbors' cars from school. I bet professors live here."

Tim agreed. "Seems like they're having a party here, though."

Arching windows lent an inquisitive air to the place, like raised eyebrows on a curious countenance.

A stained-glass sun and moon dominated the entryway. Casey pushed the doorbell. Westminster chimes sounded.

Tim pushed the doorbell. More Westminster chimes.

Mabon answered and jumped. "What are you doing here?" Sweat covered his face and darkened his shirt. His left eye twitched. He glanced over his shoulder.

He infuriates me, and I'm not sure why.

Tim said, "We should ask you that. Why'd you leave your shop?"

Mabon stumbled into a white-upholstered chair in the entry hall. "I had something to do."

I can't take this. He ran away. "Please move aside. We're here to speak to Cassandra."

He thrust both of his chins toward her. "Yeah? Well, she's not here."

"We'll wait." Casey tried to push through. His body odor made her gag.

Sparse furnishings perched atop white marble floors in the room behind him. *Not very practical in these parts. It must be freezing in here in the winter.*

Angled skylight windows in the vaulted ceilings allowed dappled sunlight to stream in. *Doesn't seem like anyone actually lives here. It's too clean.*

Mabon blocked further progress with his perspiring mass. "You need to leave now."

Tim loomed over Mabon. "Why?"

Mabon paled. "You don't scare me, you big galoot. You get out of here before I call the police."

"And tell them what, exactly? We're here to see an old friend, just like you. I'm assuming that's why you're here, right? When we started asking questions, you thought you'd pay Cassandra a call? Besides, the cops would like to talk to you anyway."

Mabon's doughy face twisted, and his jowls dripped over his perplexed jaw.

Tim's read this right, I think. What's this guy hiding?

Tim guided the girls to a white couch and sat with his arms outstretched along the back.

Mabon's mouth worked like a fish trapped on a dock. "I-I don't even know if this is her place."

Casey asked, "Why'd you come here then, huh?"

No reply.

Tim said, "We'll just have to find out together, then, won't we? By the way, Lily's dead. She had a heart attack or brain explosion or something around the same time you ran away from your shop. The police would like to ask you some questions."

"What?" Mabon gripped the wingback chair, his fingertips whitened as they dug into the upholstery.

"Dead?" He shook his head. "Are you sure she's dead?"

Tim glared. "That's what the coroner said when he pronounced her."

Casey fought off a sick feeling in her stomach. Images of Lily in her last moment flooded her memory. *Stop it. Pay attention to now.*

Mabon slumped into the chair. His mass over-filled it. He ran a hand over his balding head.

"She said she'd be dead before the end of November. I didn't think she knew what she was talking about. Guess she did have precognition. She said she heard a Banshee crying, that to her people, that was a premonition of death. A heart attack? She wasn't even thirty-five."

A woman's voice startled them. "Death doesn't discriminate. It comes for the old or the young, the rich or the poor. Death is the great equalizer."

Casey leapt to her feet. The woman appeared out of place, a Raphael amongst Picassos. Her dark, Bohemian clothes suited library stacks or gypsy caravans, not this slick, modern abode. "Dr. Krochalis, what are you doing here?"

"Paying an old, old friend a visit." She chuckled. "It's a merry meeting, though, with all of you here, too." She extended a hand to Mabon. "I don't believe we've met. I'm Dr. Krochalis. Dear Lily was a favorite student of mine."

Mabon struggled to his feet and shook her hand. "I've heard a lot about you, Lily." He gulped and blanched. "Lily spoke of you often."

Dr. Krochalis wiped her hand on her skirt after the contact. "Where's this famed Cassandra, then?"

Mabon averted his eyes and shifted his weight.

He looks like an elephant tethered at the circus. If the elephant ever realized it could free itself with the flick of a foot, there would be trouble.

He said, "I don't know where she is. The door was open when I got here. Thought I'd sit and wait."

Dr. Krochalis laughed. "So we all are guilty of squatting in Cassandra's house? My goodness, she needs to use her keys." She motioned to French doors which led to the lake. "Let's take a walk. It will be less awkward if we're not all sitting in her living room when she returns, I suppose. Besides, something in the way the wind dances across the lake calls to me."

"Me, too," Jaimie said. She shot through and bounced to the water's edge with the eagerness of a seal.

She tipped her head back and sniffed the breeze. "I agree with you, Dr. Krochalis. It's like the lake has a voice, and its waves pulse with each of my heartbeats."

Dr. Krochalis's eyes took on a misty expression as she watched Jaimie.

Tim slid the door shut after everyone exited, then held Casey's hand. "This is getting really weird."

Getting?

They kicked leaves, their breath visible puffs. The water reflected the sunset, undulating universes with each wave. Other than a splash which sent rippled circles across the lake and the crunch beneath their feet, silence reigned. Until a scream pierced their idyll.

Tim dropped Casey's hand and ran, a knight to rescue the imperiled damsel. Casey and Jaimie followed as Dr. Krochalis and Mabon huffed along behind.

The trees around the lake grew in a thicker patch, and their boughs lashed Casey's face as she burst through to the rocky shoreline. Tim stopped a foot or so ahead, breathing heavily. He held his arms in supplication. "Don't do this, Rom. Really, put down the knife."

I can't look. Still, she did. Rom held an odd knife at the base of Cassandra's neck. The point dripped blood in a rivulet along her spine.

The wild-eyed woman trembled. "Don't hurt me. Please."

Rom dragged her toward the lake, away from Tim. "You don't understand, Tim-Tim. She's in disguise. I figured that part out. She's the goddess. Right?" He rested his head against hers.

The knife-blade slipped further. Another ribbon of blood joined the first. Rom spoke into Cassandra's ear. "You said people can transcend who they were and become gods themselves. That's what I did. I'm a god, powerful. People bow before my might." His laughter yipped like a wolf.

His hair tangled around his unshaven face to frame his dangerous, wild eyes. He licked the side of Cassandra's face.

She closed her eyes and whimpered.

"It's time we show them your real form, don't you think, Goddess?" He pushed her head toward her chest and pushed her hair aside. "Now where's the zipper? I can't find it. Don't you have a zipper somewhere here?" He poked her back with the knife point until she slid to her knees.

That knife is made from bone. He has others like it stuffed in his boots and belt. I can see the handles.

Cassandra cried, her voice mad and shrill, "I'm not transcended yet. I'm not a goddess. Please. You're hurting me."

Tim advanced with slow, measured steps. "Rom, buddy, please don't hurt her."

Someone pressed three buttons on a phone. *Probably Dr. Krochalis.*

Another ran with an awkward gate in soft-soled shoes back the way they arrived.

Probably Mabon. The surface of the lake rippled behind the imperiled couple as though something sizable came from within the aquatic world to watch the drama unfold.

Rom pulled Cassandra closer to where waves moistened stones. "Stay back, Tim. I'm not going to hurt her. You'll see." He ripped at Cassandra's jacket and pressed the knife into her back. Blood welled around the injury and stained her shirt crimson.

He spoke into Cassandra's hair. "You don't have to disguise yourself from me. I know what you are. Show me. Show them." He motioned toward them, and blood flicked. "Tell me how to get this suit off so we can bask in your glory, Goddess."

Cassandra sobbed. "There's no zipper. Please listen to me. I am just a woman. That's all. Not a goddess. I misspoke when I said all that ascended master stuff to you."

Rom pulled her hair, whipping her face toward his. "Don't you lie now, just because you want to keep your secret. I know what you are, and I'm going to show them."

He flicked the knife again, and fresh blood flicked on Tim's creeping foot.

Cassandra yelped, tears streamed, and snot ran from her nose.

Casey shivered.

I don't even recognize Rom. Where's the college kid who ate ice cream with the band?

Dr. Krochalis' gentle touch startled her. She whispered, "Let's get behind those trees." She pointed. "Maybe we can surround and overwhelm him."

Casey mouthed, "Good idea." *Where are Jaimie and Mabon?*

Dr. Krochalis led the way. They snuck along the tree line and moved as quietly as they could.

Cassandra yelped.

They hid behind trunks and skulked to the next hiding place. The professor took a position midway along and pantomimed her intention. She'd block him if Rom ran her direction.

Casey peered from her hiding place to check on the drama by the lake's shore. *Nobody's wearing a death mask.* Casandra sniveled. Other than the scratches on the back of her neck and damage to her clothes, the woman appeared well. Terrified, but she'd live.

No deadly gashes or hollowed eyes terrified Casey. *I don't sense death.*

Casey stood on tip toes and whispered into Dr. Krochalis' ear, "Cassandra's going to be okay. Trust me on this. "*Oh my gosh, I'm right. Cassandra's frightened, but she's going to be okay. I am not seeing her death-face.*

"How can you know?"

I'm positive Cassandra will come out of this experience alive.

No problems on Dr. Krochalis' visage, either, and Tim appeared the picture of health. *Still don't know where Jaimie is, and I bet Mabon ran away again. Probably him I heard leaving. Even stupid Rom wears no signs of his own death.*

Chapter Thirty-Three

A Final Battle

Certainty lent Casey courage. *We might get hurt, but we'll live. We'll all live, even that murderer.* She gave the professor an unsteady smile and a thumbs-up and continued to sneak toward the shoreline where Rom held Cassandra.

She checked again. *No death faces anywhere. Yep, we'll all live through this.* She snuck, crouched, hid, then rushed to the next location. She used Tim's tense conversation with Rom as distraction. *This is like the dream we're all having where the woman with the long hair hides behind one thing and appears behind the next.* Casey fought a shiver. *That's a weird thought, but at least I know we'll survive.*

As Tim closed the distance between them, Rom backed away until the waters lapped his heels. His voice shook. "Tim, back off. I mean it. I have answers right here." He shook the mewling Cassandra. "We just need to get this costume off, and you'll see her as she truly is. She's the goddess of the moon."

Well, the moon goddess just peed herself. What can I do to get her away from Rom?

Casey grabbed a stick from the ground. *Hollow. Too light to do much damage.* She threw it into the lake. After a quiet splash, it floated.

A pale hand rose from the water and snatched it. Casey rubbed her eyes. *That was a human arm. Someone is in that frigid water right behind Rom and Cassandra.*

Rom yelled, "Back off, Tim." He worked the knife further into Cassandra's skin. The woman collapsed in his grip. She whimpered and hung limp. Her weight tugged Rom, and he hunched to maintain his grip.

Tim leapt and bowled Rom over. They struggled for the knife. They grunted and grappled in the leaves. Cassandra crawled away from their fight.

Jaimie emerged from the lake like a water spirit. Silent in the moonlight, she put a hand around Cassandra's mouth and pulled her into the water. Cassandra thrashed, but she stilled when Jaimie whispered in her ear. Brandishing the stick like a sword, Jaimie pulled Cassandra under the water. The surface calmed. The stick rose, a natural straw. The straw progressed, slow and quiet. They left few ripples to mar the lake as they passed until they reached to the further shore, away from Rom.

A thud. Tim crumpled to the ground at Rom's feet.

Bile clogged her throat. Casey slid along the mossy tree trunk and fell to her knees. She thrust her hand over her mouth and stifled her scream. *Tim!*

Blood trickled in dark streams from Tim's wounded head.

Casey's muffled screams filled her ears, and she squeezed her eyes shut.

A sharp pain bit into her neck. With a rough motion, a thick arm pulled her back against a man's musky-scented legs. *Rom.*

He pressed the knife deeper and dragged her to her feet. "Where is she?"

Casey stood still, but her voice trembled. "Rom, you don't need to do this. Please. Just calm down."

"You don't know what I need to do, Banshee. Now tell me where she went?"

Feed the crazy. "Maybe she flew back up to the sky? I think I saw a flash of light." Casey pointed through the skeletal tree branches. The clouds moved aside as though on cue and revealed a brilliant full moon.

Rom's sharp intake of breath heartened her. She said, "Wow, she is beautiful. I don't know how I didn't recognize her before. It was clever of you, Rom."

The pressure of his fingertips on her shoulder eased, and his rigid posture relaxed a bit. The knife point eased. "It was. You didn't know, did you?"

"No, I didn't know that she was the moon."

"No silly." He spoke with the measured patience of an adult to a young child. "She's not the moon. She's moonbeams walking. Beautiful and perfect. Did you see her ascend? She talked about becoming an ascended being. Remember?"

Red and blue lights bounced across the surface of the lake.

Keep him distracted.

Casey's heart battered her ribs, but she calmed her breath. A snowflake caught in her eyelashes. It melted to spill over her cheek like a tear. Casey wrapped her hand around his fist. She eased his hand down. The pressure on her neck lessened. She tilted her head, struggled with her reluctance to look into his eyes. *He could kill me with his bare hands.* "Guess she made the transition, huh? Rom, can I please have the knife? You don't need it now."

He stared as the moon played peek-a-boo through the clouds. Wind disguised approaching footsteps.

She eased his fingers open and slid the knife from his grip.

He whispered, "I didn't mean to kill her. She wouldn't listen."

"Who?"

"Red."

Chills chased up Casey's spine.

I knew he killed her. A snowflake landed on her nose. Gram used to call such snow kisses from Heaven. She closed her eyes and ignored his whiskey-thick breath. Red smiled in her imagination, whole and beautiful.

Rom whimpered. "She kept saying I was a wolf. I'm not. Not really."

He raked his hands through his scraggly hair. "Wolves do serve the moon goddess, though. That's why they sing to her. Beautiful songs." He howled low.

Hairs raised along the back of Casey's neck. *You know, I never saw my own face. I wonder if I survive this encounter with Rom? Can I see my own death? Ease my own passage?*

Rom licked his lips and said, "But see, even a someone like me who's not really a wolf needs to hunt and feed, and the moon goddess wanted blood."

Casey stepped back. He gripped her arms. His nails penetrated her winter coat. "The moon goddess hunts too, you know, and I'm her hound. I keep her prey plentiful." He bent and sniffed her. "People smell different when they're about to die, Casey. Did you know?"

Casey shook her head. "No, I didn't. How do they smell?"

"Like fear sweat." He licked his lips and sniffed the air.

"This lake is a sacred place, you know. It captures bits of her essence." His teeth glinted in the moonlight. "That's why I brought them here. When they died, they mingled with her here in these waters."

"How many?"

Rom's eyes took on a dreamy, distant appearance as he said, "I brought three women and Red here. And one dude. I chased him. He was looking for a mermaid, but I showed him a Goddess instead."

"What about Devon? Did you kill him, too?"

"That dick? Yeah, I killed him, but that was for me, not for the Goddess. He was hitting on Red and made up these vulgar memes about her when she wouldn't go out with him. 'Red Riding Hood looking good' they said. Had her in bondage wearing a cloak."

Meme? Like the one about me and the spider? "Are you sure he made them? Nursery rhymes seem kind of childish."

"Don't know what his problem was, but I introduced him to the Goddess' hound. Ripped his throat right out."

He licked his lips as though he savored the revel.

Clouds obscured the moon. Rom licked his canine teeth. "See how the lights dance across the water? Like the waves try to capture a bit of her magic." He squinted. "Wait, why are they colored like that?"

He clutched tighter. She winced.

"Did you call the police?" He gripped her hair, pulled, and struck her. Lights popped, quick flashes followed by darkness.

A voice sounded from the dark. "No, I did. Let her go. Now." Pinch-lipped, tough, and angry, Dr. Krochalis held a tree branch like a rifle.

"You idiot! Why'd you do that?"

Her breath condensed in angry clouds before her flushed face. "Why'd I call the police? To have them arrest you, of course. You are to harm no one. You didn't follow through with that, did you?"

"I did what the Goddess told me."

"Well, now you should do what I'm telling you, and let Casey go."

"Why should I?"

"Because life will go better for you if you do. You already have too much to atone for, Mr. Romine. You've visited a very dark part of your nature. You've interpreted beauty in graphic and hideous ways by shedding innocent blood."

"You don't know what you're talking about. I made masterpieces and offered them in a sacred way to a blessed being." He crushed Casey against his chest. "Want to become art, little Casey?"

A rush of adrenaline made her stomach ache, and her body throbbed with energy.

Fight or flight.

He threw back his head and howled, high-pitched this time, filled with anger and manic energy.

Her blood pounded, deafened her. She gripped his shoulders, fingers digging in. With all of her strength, she kneed him in the crotch.

He released her and doubled over with an 'oomph.' His hands clutched his personals.

She stomped on the top of his foot and bolted before he recovered.

Dr. Krochalis shattered the tree branch over his shoulders and followed Casey.

Tim burst through the naked branches followed by uniformed police officers.

While the officers arrested Rom, Tim embraced Casey. "Are you all right?"

Dr. Krochalis laughed. "Did you see her drop him? Nice placement, Ms. Adams."

Casey fought against nausea and forced a smile. "Glad the tree branch came in handy."

Two officers approached. "Follow us, please. Medics need to check you over, and we'll need statements."

Inside the ambulances, they warmed while paramedics checked for injuries. An ambulance had whisked Cassandra away, but Jaimie waited for them.

A thick blanket engulfed her slight shoulders, and although Casey's teeth chattered, Jaimie glowed, invigorated.

She said, "I saved her. Did you see? I pulled her into the lake and swam her to shore. Rom never knew what happened, did he?"

Casey shook her head, mouth ajar. "That water must have been freezing. How'd you do it?"

Jaimie shrugged. "I don't know. I just felt pulled to swim, and it all made sense from there. I felt really alive for the first time in a long time, like I was at home in the lake."

Dr. Krochalis said, "I think you were. Home, I mean."

"Like a water spirit," Jaimie said. She leaned out of the bay of the ambulance and reached toward the lake. "Yeah, that seems right. Tim, you were a defender."

Tim's jaw set. "I didn't do anything. Not really."

Dr. Krochalis picked plant debris from her hair and let it fall to the floor of the ambulance. "I disagree. I think we were a good team."

Casey and Jaimie nodded.

Dr. Krochalis said, "I have a question for you, though, Ms. Adams. How did you know Cassandra would survive?"

Casey shrugged. "She didn't look dead."

The paramedics and officers interrupted to take statements and make further checks.

Grateful for the distraction. I don't think I can talk about this with them any more tonight although I probably sound like a lunatic in my statement.

Chapter Thirty-Four

Purpose

Paramedics insisted Casey visit the hospital. Aunt Hettie and her dad rushed into the examination room. Worry lined their faces.

"My girl," Dad, clutched his keys in white-knuckled angst.

Aunt Hettie embraced her and burst into tears. "You could have died."

Casey glanced at her reflection in the window. Eyes deep-set from lack of sleep, tired but not a death prognostication. *Nah, it's not my day to die. Not today.*

Bandaged and bruised, Cassandra shuffled into Casey's room. "Hello."

Casey introduced Cassandra to her father and aunt.

"This young woman and her friends saved my life." Tears bubbled. "I owe you not only my gratitude but also an apology." She wrung her hands. "I knew the Equinox ceremony was potent, but," she cleared her throat, and her glance darted to Casey's relatives. A deep blush reddened her face. "None of us expected the reaction..."

She shuddered.

Casey studied the linoleum. "I know."

"When we talked about mastership and achieving a higher consciousness, we—I—didn't think our words would be taken so literally."

I thought hospitals were sterilized. This floor is a bit messy in the corners. "Dr. Krochalis says we have to be careful of our words because words possess the power to define us."

Cassandra sniffed into a tissue. "I'm so sorry. I never meant to cause so much trouble."

Casey considered. "Not sure it was you, actually." The woman who had used her regal stature to such advantage during the ceremony slumped beneath the strain of the night. None of the Equinox magic shone from her. *Perhaps we imagined it? Or maybe something else is involved, and it wasn't Cassandra at all.* "I'm glad you're okay."

"I already thanked your friends. Again, I'm so sorry."

She departed when a nurse came to check Casey's vitals. "Looks good," he said. "Bet you'll be headed home soon." He wished her well before he left the room.

Casey's dad and Aunt Hettie followed the nurse into the hallway to talk to the medical staff and a police officer, which left Casey alone. Her head buzzed, and her muscles ached. She kicked her feet in their over-sized, no-slip socks.

I just want to go home. She chuckled to herself. *Despite Mom, I want to go home.* A Sahara resided in her throat. *Wish I could get a drink of water.*

She slipped past her family into a hall brilliant with fluorescent lights. Antiseptic coated her palate. *I need a water fountain. There must be one around here somewhere.*

An old woman peered from a nearby room. "Excuse me, could you please help us?" Her voice lilted with an Irish accent.

Nobody else walked the hallway. "I'm sorry, Ma'am. I'm a patient. I don't think I can help."

The woman's cataract-clouded eyes crinkled at the corners as she squinted. "Actually, you're exactly who we need." She reached a weathered and trembling hand to Casey and pulled.

Casey stepped into the room. An old man lay on an adjustable bed, gasping with noisy, shallow breaths, his frail body mummified, gray and withered. *There's no doubt. He's dying.* Tears sprung and fell, and a moaning grew in her ears and escaped through her lips.

Casey covered her mouth and turned away. "I'm sorry," she sobbed. "I can't help you."

The old woman grabbed and patted Casey's bruised hands. A thin trickle of tears made a silent progression into the old woman's wrinkles.

"You are helping, dear. Don't you see? It makes dying easier knowing your passage is mourned."

The woman held the old man's arthritic hands. "My tears are as dry as my wrinkled skin. Your young empathy helps us both. Eases the transition."

The image blurred, awash with tears. *Clears the passage?* Grief enveloped Casey, suffocated and crushed her. She knelt beside the man's bed and held the lady's hand. *Every life is precious. I understand.* The heart monitor alarms screamed. A line smoothed the hills and peaks of the screen.

The old woman kissed her husband goodbye and wrapped Casey in a hug. "Thank you for caring, little Washer Woman," She whispered and kissed Casey's cheek.

She'll be joining her husband within a year.

As though reading her thoughts, the old woman said, "See, you helped. You led the way." She swiped her eyes. "Maybe you'll help my passage when the time comes, too? I'd like that."

Casey bit her lip to stop its tremble. "If I can."

The old woman gave her arm a squeeze as nurses swept into the room. Casey and the woman, Mrs. McGill—*Why do I know her name?*—were escorted out.

Mrs. McGill's smile deepened the crevices in her face. She resembled an aged apple doll, plump, kind, and comforting.

"I didn't think we'd see one of your kind here in America, but I guess your kin are all over. I'm so glad you came." She patted Casey's hand.

Casey mopped her tears with the edge of her hem. "My kin?"

Mrs. McGill patted Casey's arm with wizened hands. "You don't know, do you? In my country, you're called Washer Woman. You scrub out the stains of our sins with your tears and give warning so we can prepare for a loss."

What?

"To some, you are Banshee."

Banshee? Rom called me that.

"Don't you see, my dear? Your tears clean the path to the next world. Your compassion helps us on our way."

Someone to open the door and point the way.

Chapter Thirty Five

A Confrontation

Casey's father carried Casey's plastic "personal" hospital bag. Aunt Hettie held a vase of carnations and a bouquet of "get well" helium balloons. Bandaged and bruised, Tim joined their parade. He'd extended a friendly hand to her father and Aunt Hettie, and they seemed to like him. A transportation volunteer pushed Casey in a wheelchair.

"I don't understand why they won't let me walk," Casey complained.

"Hospital policy." The volunteer inclined his head toward Tim. "You should probably be in a chair yourself, buddy."

Tim snorted. "I'm good. Thanks though."

Dad patted her arm. "Just be glad you're coming home. Who cares how you get there? The kids will be going out of their mind."

Wonder what Mom'll think. Casey nodded to the people she met said prayers for those she knew would die soon. Their labored breath calmed with her passage, and tension melted from their faces. Casey closed her eyes, amazed. *I can make dying easier.*

Tim's mom and brother met them outside. She pulled her son's face to her and kissed until he laughed. Tommy, decked out in native-inspired beadwork, remained stoic. "Thank the Great Spirit you're all alive."

Tim's mom kissed Casey, at a loss for words.

They made introductions.

On the car ride, Aunt Hettie cracked a crooked smile. "So, Tim's super cute."

Casey chuckled. "He really is."

At home, the kids crushed Casey with hugs. "I missed you crazies," Casey gushed.

"We missed you more!" they sang in unison. Rachel displayed the vase of flowers on the kitchen table, and Malcolm played with the balloons. Casey kissed her sibling and left them in the kitchen.

"Stay here, okay? Promise?"

The kids nodded, suddenly sober.

"And no spying. "Casey squinted, lips pressed into a serious line. "I'm not joking."

"Okay."

Before fear could shake her resolve, Casey marched into the living room. Mother reposed on the sofa, her double chin set in stubborn determination, eyes narrowed with distrust.

"Hello, Mother."

"Casey." No expression of concern. No tearful reunion. No "you saved lives" or "you could have died." Just her name cold in her mother's mouth.

Casey pushed aside her hurt and concentrated on her mother. "I have something important to tell you, and you need to listen. You need help. Professional help. Mental illness is an illness, and you need to treat it, just like you treat any other disease."

Her father placed a hand on Casey's shoulder. "Now Casey..."

She put her hand up. "Daddy, don't interrupt, please."

His mouth hung silent.

"Listen to me, Mother. What I'm saying is you need to treat this or it won't get better. You need to take medicine every day, not just when you're feeling bad."

Her mother pinched her lips tight.

Casey stepped closer. "I know this isn't easy to hear, but Mom, I'm saying it because we love you. This is no way to live. The kids want their mother back, not—" Casey motioned. "Someone too selfish to care about them or herself." Casey's voice cracked. "Please, Momma. We love you."

Her mother balled her hands into fists.

"What if I don't want that kind of help? You don't know what I'm going through."

Casey envisioned possible outcomes. Without knowing why, she knew. "Then, my dear mother, you will die. Probably by suicide. You've thought about it, haven't you? Planned it. How you'd take your own life?"

Her mother gasped. Her voice gushed like a deflating tire. "How dare you?"

Casey examined the sad explorations she instinctively knew her mother had undertaken. "Daddy might not be able to find you the next time you make a hotel reservation."

Her mother turned a livid expression on her father.

Her father's face froze. "I never said a word."

"No, Daddy didn't say anything. You made reservations and ordered what you thought would be your last meal. Fettuccini Alfredo. Two bottles of white wine. Tiramisu for dessert. All accompanied by every pill you'd hoarded for over three months."

Aunt Hettie gasped. "My God. You didn't, did you?" She grabbed Dad's arm. "Did she?"

His pale face resembled granite, but he inclined his chin.

Her mother rose in a red-faced rage and towered over Casey.

Spittle churned within her enraged mouth and sprayed with each word. "You little bitch! You have no idea what you're talking about?"

Casey ignored her natural terror of her mother's changeable rages. Instead, she traversed deeper into the sorrow that shrouded her mother.

"Don't I? Do you deny the razor blades you hide in your bubble bath container and your fantasy of turning the water a frothy garnet color?"

Her head ached as she saw the ways her mother planned to die.

"The accidental car crash over Gulliver's Ridge you scoped out? Why brake? Hover for a few glorious seconds before gravity called you home." Casey pointed to the seat cushion vacated by her mother. "Or the unregistered gun you've hidden under that cushion?"

Her mother's mouth popped with apoplectic turmoil. She reached to Casey's father, but he remained rooted, uncharacteristically unmoved by her tears.

Aunt Hettie tore the cushions from the couch and recoiled from the .22 caliber pistol slid between the arm and the back.

I just knew. It's all true.

Her mother wheeled, vulnerable and dangerous, a mixture of tears and terror.

"Why are you doing this to me?"

Tears bit at Casey's eyes.

"Because Mom, if I don't, you'll die.

"You keep whistling up a storm, and soon Death's going to bring the typhoon that will take you home. I can see many ways for your death to visit. Within a year if you don't get help. So this may seem mean, but I have to tell you. Even if you don't believe me, which would make you foolish. And if I can help you, I will, even if you hate me for it."

Aunt Hettie stifled sobs as Dad edged into the room and fell at Mom's feet. "We'll always be here for you, darling. Casey's right, though. We need to get some help."

Some of the haze lifted from her mother's body, as she shed a gauzy layer of her shroud. Although it still rested on her, Casey knew if her mother sought the needed help, she'd leave her suicide veil behind.

Chapter Thirty-Six

In Conclusion

School concluded for the semester in a whirl of finals and caffeine.

Casey received an email from the Dean. *What could this be?* Casey worried herself into hives until she received a text message from Jaimie.

"I'm supposed to see the Dean."

Casey responded. "Me, too."

The phone jingled again. Tim sent a text. "Look, I hope I'm not in any trouble, but I've been summoned to the Dean's office. If I don't come out alive, just know I love you."

I love you? Tim said he loves me? Of course, he could mean it as a joke, like "I love you, Bro."

Casey scratched her hives. *What if he really means it? Do I love him, too?* Casey stumbled through her foggy thoughts to meet Jaimie.

They hugged. Jaimie asked, "What's wrong? Well, besides the whole Dean's summons thing."

Casey showed Tim's message to Jaimie who smirked. "What do you think it means?"

Casey considered. "I don't know, but it sure seems odd."

"Odd? I don't think it seems odd at all. He's been goo-goo eyed for you since he first met you." She bumped her shoulder into Casey, like a playful pup.

They linked arms as they made their way to the Dean's office. Jaimie giggled. "We're off to see the Wizard."

"Casey!" Tim's deep voice reverberated through her chest. He rushed to catch up. "Did you come to see me to the gallows?" He touched his gloved fingertip to the edge of her nose.

Casey ducked her head. "We've been summoned, too."

"Hop on in here, Tim-man. Let's follow the Yellow Cobblestone Road." She pointed to the stone pathway and laughed. Tim chuckled and offered Casey his arm. They marched like the Oz gang.

A secretary greeted them. "He'll be with you in just a minute. Please help yourself to coffee."

She watched Jaimie's quiver, pursed her lips, and returned her attention to her computer screen. She muttered, "Unless you don't need any more caffeine."

Sunlight streamed through a stained-glass window topper, transforming the polished wood of the office with its fairy lights.

Casey ran her fingers through a pretty golden shade. *I wonder if this is the end of my collegiate career?*

The intercom buzzed, and the secretary pulled her glasses from her face, allowing them to dangle from a chain about her neck. "He'll see you now." She swept her hand toward a heavy oaken door. "That way."

"Thanks," Casey said, feeling less thankful than nervous.

Drs. Krochalis and Bridges greeted them at the door. Dr. Krochalis' smile broadened her already wide face. "Casey, Jaimie, Tim! Glad you're here." She turned to the dean. "Dr. Rosen, these are the academias of whom we told you." She turned to them as though making introductions at a cocktail party. "This is Dean Julia Rosen."

A smile fought to control Dr. Rosen's studied academia-inspired features. "Welcome to my office. I've heard a great deal about you." She stood and extended a wizened hand to each of them. "Not only are you excellent students, the school and I owe you a great debt. I understand you were of more help in bringing Mr. Romine to justice than either or campus or local police. For that, I wanted to thank and commend you."

Not in trouble, then. Thank heavens for that.

Tim seemed to agree.

He covertly grasped and squeezed Casey's hand. She squeezed back. Casey studied the feet of the dean's large desk. She slipped into introverted ways, easier than eye contact.

She cleared her throat, steeled for speech. "Dr. Krochalis deserves a lot of credit, too. She tried to talk Rom down, and boy..." she stole a glance at Dr. Krochalis' smiling face, "...can she swing a mean branch."

The Dean asked them to recount the events and plumbed their knowledge of the Equinox Ceremony. "I don't believe that will be an activity resumed in the future."

Dr. Krochalis cleared her throat and shifted her weight from one ballerina flat to the other. "Well, it was meant as an exploration of tribal customs and self-awareness."

"Be that as it may," the Dean's eyebrows rose, "the psychological effects on our students are too unpredictable. Dr. Bridges and I agree on that point. In the future, students will have to investigate such customs on their own, and off of campus property."

Dr. Krochalis and Dr. Bridges exchanged a weighty stare, but Dr. Krochalis nodded. "In truth, the alumna who organized the ceremony these past seven years has passed away, and her business partner, Mr. Mabon, is under arrest."

Casey's head snapped up.

Dr. Krochalis nodded. "Something about selling and using mind-altering drugs."

Jaimie chewed the inside of her cheek as though hesitant to speak. "What about Cassandra?"

Dr. Krochalis said, "Cassandra was a friend of Lily's. Seems she is going on a retreat. Tibet, I think it is. Finds the need to center and explore the purpose of her existence. She said she felt a bit lost after all that happened."

Jaimie sighed. "I'm just glad she's all right."

Dr. Krochalis agreed. "It looked pretty dire for her, indeed, when Mr. Romine had that miserable bone knife to her throat." She looked sideways at Casey. "However, she made it through."

Jaimie locked eyes with Dr. Bridges. "I wonder if you can help a friend of ours. Ryan. He also attended the ceremony, and now he's obsessed with painting. Won't even stop to eat or care for himself."

Dr. Bridges removed and wiped his spectacles. "I do believe I know of the gentleman in question. I'm not a psychiatrist, but I know some esteemed members of the field. Perhaps we can visit your friend's dorm together during the afternoon break?"

Jaimie nodded. A waterfall of relief washed over her features.

The dean shook their hands again, clapping a hand on each of their shoulders. "If there's ever something like this happening, you must come to me." She narrowed her eyes. "Of course, nothing like this should ever happen again."

Tim wrapped Casey's hand in his as they made their way out the door. Before she crossed the threshold, though, Dr. Rosen called her name. "Ms. Adams, one moment more, if you don't mind?"

Oh no. Now what?

Tim smiled down at her. "I'll be right out here with Jaimie. We'll get coffees after, okay?"

Casey nodded and tried to offer a smile, but she failed the attempt.

Dr. Rosen motioned to a burgundy leather armchair. "Please have a seat. there's one other matter I needed to discuss with you." She shuffled some papers. "Some time earlier in October, I understand you were a victim of cyber-bullying."

Casey shifted in the seat, uncomfortable. *Frighten Miss Casey away.*

The dean continued. "Believe it or not, we strive for a peaceful environment for our students, one safe from such attacks. We've discovered the perpetrator. He'll not be making any other clever images to post in cyberspace."

Casey swallowed. *Because he's dead.* "Excuse me, was it Devon Dare?"

Dr. Rosen sniffed with surprise. "Yes, it was indeed Devon Dare." She studied Casey a moment. "I thought you'd want to know. I am sorry we couldn't stop the images earlier."

If you had, Devon might still be alive. He'd have never made his Red image. "Thanks," Casey said instead. *Enough guilt in this world without piling on more.*

Another handshake with the dean. "Please come to me if you have any other problems. That's why I'm here."

"Thank you," Casey said again, unsure what else to say.

She joined Tim and Jaimie. They walked to the coffee shop where the friends shared their accomplishments over piping-hot mugs of hot buttered lattes. While they compared grades, Casey thought of Rachel and Malcolm. They worked hard these nine weeks. *We'll have a popcorn party when their report cards come in.*

She blew on the foam in her mug. The cream created a swirled design. *Looks like a feather.* She smiled at Tim. "How is your brother doing?"

Tim winked. "Better now that they are working on the Native American section in history. He's been providing the teacher with examples of their crafts and correcting his lectures."

They laughed. Outside the snug shop, snow formed a thick blanket over the campus. "I think he's going to be okay. It's like he's passionate, but not as crazed as before," Tim said.

Jaimie sighed. "Wish it was the same for Ryan."

Casey touched her hand. "Maybe it will be. Dr. Bridges said he'd meet with him and recommend him to some colleagues."

Jaimie glanced at her phone. "I have to leave in about fifteen minutes to meet him. Casey, will you come? You can see if he—um—looks right."

Casey grabbed Jaimie's hand. "Sure."

Tim set a flyer from Steel City Art Gallery on the table. "Speaking of Ryan. Check out who's got a show."

Ryan's art revisited dark dreams.

Casey shuddered at the image of a wolf howling at a glorious woman clad in moonshine.

Jaimie squinted at an image of the moon shimmering on the school's lake. "Want to go this Saturday?"

Casey stared at a woman clad in a white nightgown so like her own. She led souls to a cemetery. She shivered. *I hate that nightgown now.*

Tim noticed her discomfort. He took her hand and pressed it to his lips. "Can't, Jaimester. I'm taking this lady on an actual, honest to God, reservations and everything, date."

"Oh yeah, I forgot," Jaimie blushed. "Not getting in the way of that."

The floor moved with Jaimie's constant fidgeting. "Maybe we could go Sunday, though? They have a matinee."

"Sure," Tim said.

Jaimie studied the pictures and bit her lip. "Guess it's a matter of time before he's kicked off campus. He's skinny as a skeleton since he doesn't sleep or eat or anything, but at least he has 'found his muse.'"

She swiped her tears before they fell. "I hope he'll be successful and happy."

Casey squeezed Jaimie's hand. "I hope he'll be successful, too. It's a shame his muse is such a slave driver. Art'll kill him if he's not careful."

Jaimie's eyes widened with alarm.

Casey rushed to add, "Figurative speech, of course."

Tim tapped the tops of their hands. "See what Dr. Bridges has to say."

They sipped from their drinks. Citrusy nutmeg coated Casey's teeth.

"Red's memorial service will be Monday in the school chapel," Jaimie said.

"We'll be there," Casey answered.

None of us talk about Rom any more, not since he was sent to that insane asylum upstate. She rubbed her arms where his nails had ripped into her.

He dumped the bodies of Devon, Annamarie, and two other women by the lake, sacrifices to his crazy idea.

Casey fought a glut of tears back to another corner of her mind to explore later. *Worst of all, he confessed to pushing Jaimie's brother into the lake. He said his sister waited at the bottom, in the sludge. He watched James die. I somehow knew it.*

Jaimie offered a wobbly smile. "By the way, I'm changing my major to Environmental Sciences."

Casey raised her eyebrows. "That's a great fit. Will you specialize in water environments?"

Jaimie's laughter musical, like waves along a sandy shore. "Of course."

Tim sat back in his chair.

Look at those strong arms. I love when he holds me.

He caught her and wiggled his eyebrows. She ducked her head, blushed, then peeked up with an imitating eyebrow wiggle.

Jaimie hid a giggle behind her coffee cup. "You two are so cute! Gosh, Casey, I remember how shy you were when I first met you. You barely kept eye contact when people talked to you back then."

"I think this experience changed us all."

They all nodded and fell silent.

Casey asked, "Do you still dream of her?"

They required no clarification. "Sometimes," Jaimie said.

Tim closed his eyes as though he wished to forget but nodded. "Not as much now, but she's still there, hiding behind thoughts."

Casey ran a finger through some spilled sugar and drew an outline of an eye. "Disappearing and reappearing. She's always there now, isn't she?"

They nodded again and took long sips of their drinks.

Tim patted his mustache with a paper napkin. "Well, Jaimie, you're not the only one who's found a new calling. No more finance major for me. I'm studying Criminal Justice."

Jaimie tipped her cup in tribute. "You've got the chops for it, that's for sure."

"My knight in shining armor." Casey nestled beside him and rested her head on his chest.

His heart beat strong and steady, prepared for a marathon symphony. "Guess we all embrace our truest selves." She wiped her lips with a paper napkin.

"I declared my major. Psychology. I'm going into end of life counselling."

About the Author

Kerry E. B. Black lives along a fog-enshrouded river outside the land where George A. Romero's Dead dawned.

She writes an eclectic mix of short stories, poetry, non-fiction, flash fiction, dancing with words to create nightmarish stories which dip into the universality of fear. Some of her works have crept into anthologies, and she enjoys working with www.gamesomniverse.com.

Kerry is wife to a good man, as well as a mom to 5 delightful urchins and their family menagerie.

Follow her online

www.facebook.com/authorKerryE.B.Black
www,twitter.com/BlackKerryblick
www,kerrylizblack.wordpress.com
www.goodreads.com/author/show/7874880.Kerry_E_B_Black

turn the page for a special preview of

Season of Sorrows

~ Esoteric Equinox - Book II ~

---

coming soon from

Kerry E. B. Black

AND RHETASKEW PUBLISHING

Chapter One

A Surprise Homecoming

THE DREAMS OF the witch came less frequently, but Casey continued to deal with the visions. Since life and death continued without her permission, she played her unlooked-for part.

Since the autumn equinox ceremony, Casey Adams could tell if someone was about to die, and she mourned for them. Her tears eased their passage to their next existence.

As the sun rose, she stretched away the night's grip and readied for the day. "Rise and shine, Sweet peas," she called to her siblings.

"Already up, Sleepy Head." Her brother Malcolm zoomed through the hallway clad in a superhero cape and mask.

"Hey, slow down, Crazy Man." Casey scooped him into a hug as he rushed by. "You can't go to school wearing a cape and mask. Teacher would not approve."

He wiggled free and placed hands on his squared hips. "Yeah, but what if a bad guy shows up at school? They'll be glad a superhero is there if a bad guy shows up. I can stop him if I have my cape and mask, but if I don't, what then?"

Casey ruffled his hair. "We'll have to take our chances, I guess. Besides, you're pretty tough in your civie clothes, you know."

He puffed out his thin chest. "Darned right."

Casey wiped her upper lip to disguise a smile. "Breakfast in five, okay?"

"What're we having today? Cereal?" Rachel yawned in her doorway.

"Only the finest grains for you." Casey kissed her sister's cheek. "And milk. Mustn't forget the milk."

They laughed and set to the morning's preparations. Hair brushes and lip gloss littered the sink. The toothpaste leaked from its uncapped tube.

Casey sighed and tidied as she went through the daily routine. Pick up and rehang a towel. Straighten the tub mat. Close the shower curtain.

At least she could make noise, though, with Mom away. When Mom was home, they scampered about like mice all day long, afraid to wake the dragon's wrath.

As she carried their night clothes to the laundry basket, Casey froze. Raised voices downstairs.

Dad and a woman. Casey strained. Not Mom. Thank goodness. Aunt Hettie! But why did she sound upset?

With a leaden weight in her stomach, Casey descended to peek into the kitchen.

Dad sat in his seat, dejected head in his aging hands. Aunt Hettie paced. "Where would she have gone?"

Dad shook his head. Gray dulled his locks. "I don't know. Let me think, okay? I bet she'll be home here in a couple."

Home? Did Mom leave the treatment center?

Aunt Hettie threw her hands into the air. "What's the point of intense therapy if she walks away from it? How'd she get out?"

"I don't know, Hettie. It's not like she was a prisoner. She probably put on her coat and walked out the door. How're they supposed to know if she's a patient or a visitor?"

Sure don't want to be here for Mom's homecoming.

Heart pounding, Casey rushed back upstairs to hurry her siblings. "We'll get breakfast on the way. I'm driving you to school today."

Rachel tried to hide a blush brush beneath a face cloth. "Won't that make you late for school? What's going on?"

Malcolm thrust his chin into a heroic pose. "Yeah, is there trouble about?"

Casey grabbed their backpacks and coats. "Just want to spend time with you. Now hurry." She tossed their shoes to them.

Malcolm struggled with his laces. Casey stooped and tied them for him.

Malcolm pouted. "Hey, I can do it."

The screen door slammed downstairs.

Hopefully, that's Aunt Hettie on her way to her shift at the diner and not Mom popping by.

Casey tried to ignore her thundering worries. She smiled at her brother. "I know you can, but now it's done. Two perfect, double-knotted bows. See? Now let's get going." She shoved her arms through her coat sleeves, careful of the ripped lining, grabbed her purse, and sprinted down the stairs. "I'll beat you both to the car!"

Malcolm scrambled to catch her. Rachel brought up the rear, disinterested in the outcome of the race.

Only Dad sat at the kitchen table. "Bye, Dad!" Casey kissed his cheeks as she passed. "I'm driving the kids today.

Malcolm mimicked Casey's exit while Rachel swept through in a more stately fashion.

Casey flung open the door to leave.

She and her siblings gasped. Their Mom's bulk blocked their exit. A winter wind swirled her hair about her face like Medusa's snakes. The wind and the myth froze them in place until Mom narrowed her eyes and a dangerous line formed between her brows.

"And where do you think you're going?"

* * *

WWW.RHETORICASKEW.COM